In the Pursuit of Charity
a prequel

Alexandria Sure

In the Pursuit of Charity

Alexandria Sure

ISBN 978-0-9991004-0-0

To all those people who second-guess themselves.

No act of kindness, however small, is ever wasted.

~ aesop

CHAPTER 1

Linc James had a life decision to make and thinking about it was preventing him from getting much sleep. Bored with watching the ceiling, he dressed in his faded grey sweats and a 'Born to Swim' long-sleeved tee shirt that wasn't quite long enough in the sleeve for his extra-long limbs. He walked from the dark bedroom to the unlit kitchen and opened the refrigerator.

Linc's swimming career ended two weeks ago, but years of getting up early for swim practice was a habit not easily changed. Once on the sofa in the living room, Linc played *Call of Duty* and ate oatmeal by the glow of the TV. His plan was to go through the day like it was any other and hope that by the end there'd be clarity.

He brushed his teeth and swished his mouthwash, ignoring his hair. As he made his way to the front door, he glanced at the clock on the wall.

"Shit! Three forty-five."

You're early.

He closed the door and walked toward the IM building.

Excellent. Alone with your thoughts again.

Linc lived off-campus in a house his parents purchased the year he started at Michigan State. It was a few blocks from everything, which made it easy to walk everywhere.

Dude, you're almost out of here. Are you staying?

He started jogging. The need to feel water all over his body grew, as did the anticipation of the delight that would come from leaving his thoughts on dry land. The sooner Linc submerged in the pool, the sooner he could escape.

Linc smiled as he ran passed Beaumont Tower. He'd miss State. He'd miss his teammates, too. His best friends weren't staying in East Lansing after graduation, and Becks had left sooner than expected.

He stopped at the top step of the IM building to turn and look over the campus.

Everything would be different.

CHAPTER 2

Linc's last kick propelled him chest-high across the plane of water toward the wall. He lay back with his eyes closed and relaxed into the comfort of the water while the movement in the pool settled.The harsh trill of a whistle made Linc jump. His eyes flew open, and his legs dropped down below him.

Shit! Should've known. Izzie The Enforcer. Bustin' balls before sunrise.

Everyone called Izzie "The Enforcer" because she'd happily bust any swimmer's balls without consideration for who might be around. Linc removed his goggles and peeled off his cap as she took her usual spot at the end of the bleachers.

"Please explain why we've had to listen to you bitch for the last four years about morning practices, and now that the season's over, you're in the pool before team practice is even scheduled to start."

"Habit," Linc said, as he climbed out of the pool. Water ran over the hard muscles of his lanky body. He rubbed his hands across his face and through his hair. Most of his life had been spent in a pool or standing next to one.

"What'd you say?" Izzie looked up from her clipboard.

"It's a habit to be here early in the morning."

She nodded and returned to reviewing the stack of papers on her clipboard.

"Iz." Linc sat on the diving block across from the assistant coach.

"Huh?"

"Izzie?" Linc waited for her to look up, and when she did, she placed the clipboard on the bench beside her. "My kick was off. We already know that, but I think I pressed out too wide, too."

"Linc."

"I know we've talk about this, but I keep replaying every second of the race, and if I–"

"Linc. Stop." She leaned forward and rested her forearms on her knees. "It's over."

He looked down at the small pool of water collecting on the tile under his feet. "I was supposed to–"

"Were you?" Izzie sat up straight. "Who said?"

Linc scanned the pool to avoid looking her in the eye. Instead, he honed in on the 1956 championship banner. This was supposed to have been the year a new banner would hang. He had failed everyone.

"I let everyone down."

Dude, hold it together.

This was the first time Linc had voiced the words, even though he had been playing them on repeat since disqualifying his relay team from their final race eleven days and thirteen hours ago.

"Linc, this is all just one part of your life journey." She waved her hands around the pool, "You're going to have different experiences. Some good, and some not so good. The thing is, this is your path. When you're doing what you're meant to do, you can't let anyone down."

Izzie picked up her clipboard to continue where she left off. Linc watched the ripples reflecting sparkles of light off the water.

Minutes passed, and Linc switched gears. "Guess what I thought about today?"

"Oh, shit. There's no telling?"

"Remember that day I got a new towel every time I got out of the pool, and you went nuts on me?"

"I'd challenge 'went nuts', but yeah."

Linc smiled at Izzie's air quotes.

"I think it was also the same day we asked you if you wanted us to pick up our own mats after warm-up, and you said, 'No, I enjoy walking around picking up after you. Of course, pick up your own damn mats.' It was the same practice when you told us it didn't matter if we came from money or had influential parents because 'the water doesn't care, and neither do I.'" He ran his finger along the band of his goggles. "I remember thinking, 'who is this assistant coach at a state college telling me anything? I'll receive more money for graduation than she'll make in a whole year.'"

"Ouch." Izzie held her heart.

"I was an asshole."

"Was? Huh."

"I'm probably still an asshole, but I'm really working on being a better person." Linc moved to sit next to Izzie. "You've always been here for me. Whether I needed support or an ass kicking, you've been here. For all of us. And you've never asked for anything in return."

"That's the job, Linc. Four years ago, when you walked onto this pool deck thinking you owned the world, I couldn't imagine you receiving an offer to stay on as a swim coach. What you see in me and Coach, we see in you."

Linc's shoulders slumped from the weight of her words. It took swimmers time to figure out that as much of an 'enforcer' Izzie was, she was also a supporter. One force would've never been as effective without the other. She had more faith in Linc than he did, and it scared him.

Izzie glanced at the clock. "Practice is starting. We could use a timekeeper."

"Are they swimming outside today?"

"Warm-ups are outside. Drills are in here. Divers are practicing out there, too."

Linc and Izzie waited in the hallway as swimmers trickled out of the locker room and headed outside. The warmth of the water and the chill of the morning air collided over the pool and created a swirl of ghostly fog.

Shit, I'm glad I don't have to get in there this morning.

Izzie leaned in. "I wasn't going to ask, but have you given the offer anymore thought?"

"I haven't thought of much else."

"Good. Do you know why the offer was written for next season?"

"So I could graduate first?"

"Sure, but Coach could have started you at an 'in-training' position." Izzie looked out at the pool. "He wanted you to have a drying off period."

Linc waited for her to continue.

"You've been in the pool since second grade. Your entire life has been the water. After the race, he felt you needed time to wrap your head around the loss and spend some time on dry land."

Okay, shit! I get it. Deal with this.

Izzie smiled. "Understand?"

He nodded and forced a small smile.

The door to the locker room flew open and banged against the wall. Two laughing seniors walked out, then froze when they saw Izzie.

"Shit!" one of them declared.

Izzie smiled at them. "Exactly. How nice of the two of you to volunteer as timekeepers for the day. Linc, your services are no longer needed. Thank you."

She winked at Linc as his teammates lowered their heads and skulked by. He knew they had come to make fun of the swimmers who were still in training. Like Linc, their final season had come to an end, but they weren't quite ready to let it go either.

Izzie nudged Linc. "Any plans for the day?"

"I have a date later." He rolled his eyes. "Harrison set it up."

"Oh Christ! You're either really brave or really stupid. Let me know how it goes."

Stupid.

Unlike his friends, who took advantage of the reactions chicks had to their bodies from their hours spent in the pool and gym, he regretted the fact that there had been a short string of conquests after his last breakup. One-night stands hadn't been the plan with any of them, but waking up the next morning always shined a light on his lack of interest. Harrison had guaranteed this one would be different.

CHAPTER 3

Seriously? What is it about me that made my friends think I would be interested in this chick from Friendship Circle? What a strange name for a street. Hi, my name is Linc, and I live on Friendship Circle. It doesn't even work for a guy. Shit, did she just ask me a question? Shit, what's her name again?

Harrison had suggested the local twenty-four hour greasy spoon taken over by students years ago; the one that refused to play anything but the original fifteen classic rock songs that came with the joint when it had opened. A diner wasn't a great place for a first date, and Linc had argued the noise would make it difficult to carry on a conversation. Both of his best friends had laughed at his comment.

"What?" Linc shifted forward in his seat and placed his arms on the table.

The girl with caked-on makeup and hair pulled into a tight bun, who sat across from him in the booth, giggled. She began speaking again, but this time Linc was determined to follow what she was saying.

"Okay, so. The cheerleaders sort of treat us..."

Wait. What's her name? I can't call her Friendship Circle all night. Such a dumb ass name for a street. I bet some guy named it that to get laid. I'm going to beat the shit out of Harrison for this date. What the hell? Did I miss another question?

"Uh huh." Linc slid his hand down front of his shirt.

"Exactly! See, I knew I was right."

I should get a green one of these. I wonder what other colors are available. Come on. Where's the food?

A quick affirmation was all it took to send Friendship Circle off to the races in conversation with herself. Linc nodded when she took a breath. Eye contact kept the story going, but if she paused at any point with another question, he'd be so busted.

"HA! Overtime...exactly like I said. Pay up!"

Linc closed his fists to keep from turning around to catch a glimpse of the woman talking basketball behind him. His seat lifted as someone slid in behind him, bringing an air of sweetness, a combination of fruit and flowers and sugar water.

"I'd say Arizona did an excellent job at shutting down Mercer and Padgett. As I may have mentioned, prior to you placing your bet. Pay up!"

The red pleather groaned as Linc slid his arm across the back of the booth to steal a look at the chick talking about last night's playoff game. His fingers glided over a crack in the pleather where students of years past no doubt had attempted to peer at one another.

"You got lucky on this one."

Linc smiled at the annoyance in the guy's voice. The woman's knowing laugh hit Linc with the same joy as a child handed cotton candy at the fair. It was a laugh without restraint or regard for who was around. It reminded Linc of he and his sister laughing, and their mom trying to rein in Grace saying it wasn't ladylike. Grace loved people to watch, so his mom's argument only made his sister laugh louder.

Linc laughed. Friendship Circle cocked her head and gave him a look of disgust. "I didn't think it was very funny, Linc. Perhaps, I didn't explain our side clearly enough."

"I'm sorry. I must have misunderstood. Go for it."

She glanced down and smiled wildly. When she slowly looked up, she batted her eyes and reached over the table to touch Linc's forearm.

Excellent. Boney ice cube fingers.

"It's okay. The whole cheer and dance squad dynamic does get confusing. I'll go slower."

And with that, Friendship Circle was off on another tangent Linc couldn't care five shits about.

"I'd call it total IMPLOSION of your team."

Just like that, Linc was sucked back into the conversation behind him. Another grin spread across his face. Implosion was the exact same word he had used when he had watched the game. His intense dislike for Kentucky, combined with his friend Asker's reverence for the team, made for a loud night of shit talking.

"Thank you very much. Always a pleasure."

As the waitress set plates in front of Linc and his date, she asked if they needed anything else. All he wanted to do was switch seats. Talking basketball sounded like much more fun than being talked at by his date.

"I said no tomato or onion," Friendship Circle stated. She slid her plate toward the edge of the table. "Clearly, there's a slice of both on the lettuce. Am I correct?"

"I apologize."

"Just don't put it on the burger," Linc advised, with a wink at the waitress.

"My instructions were clear. I don't even want them on my plate!" She sat back against the booth with her arms crossed and a pout on her overly made-up face.

Linc dropped his burger on the plate and looked at the waitress, confident his disbelief was evident. The waitress silently removed the plate and returned to the kitchen.

She's in for way more than just the removal of a tomato and onion slice. This chick is ridiculous.

Linc felt the seat give as someone relieved it of their weight.

Laughter drew Linc back in his seat to catch the rest of the conversation behind him. Friendship Circle sat scrolling through her phone.

"I can't believe she called that game."

"She knows her shit. Have you ever watched a game with her?"

Linc leaned back to hear better.

Who is this chick?

"My roommate went home for the weekend. Want to watch a movie after this?"

Linc flinched when Friendship Circle touched his arm. He half nodded, not wanting to miss anything behind him.

A third male voice piped in. "I heard she goes to some of State's practices. Scouts for them, too."

That's hot.

"That's kind of hot," one of the guys in the booth said. Linc bobbed his head in agreement.

"It would be, if she wasn't huge."

"Oh, come on, you'd fuck her."

"I don't do livestock."

The waitress gently placed a new plate in front of Friendship Circle and waited for more abuse.

"Finally!" Friendship Circle responded.

Linc needed to get away from this rude chick. "Check, please."

"I haven't eaten yet."

"Ma'am. Could we get boxes and the check? I need to get out of here." The waitress smirked at Linc knowingly and darted off with the plates.

Friendship Circle watched the waitress flee. "Are you going to tell me what's going on?"

"Yeah, I am just not feeling that well. I think we should cut the night short. You can eat at home."

Boxed dinners and the check made it to the table as Friendship Circle finished reapplying her caked-on lipstick. Linc dropped money on the table. He included a generous tip to cover his date's lack of manners.

This is the longest seven-minute drive ever. Does this chick ever stop yapping? I'm going to jack Harrison up for this shit. Do I want to watch a movie? Are you kidding me? What I want to do is drop kick your ass off to the curb.

"Ready?" Linc asked, as he slipped the car into park. He placed the to-go container in Friendship Circle's hand and shuddered as her eyes combed over him.

"Sur–" Friendship Circle started when Linc opened the passenger door. "Are you positive you don't want to come in and hang out? Watch a movie or, you know, whatever?"

Linc suppressed his desire to laugh in her face. "Look, I don't think this is going to happen."

"Oh. Okay," she said, blinking repeatedly.

"Have a good night," Linc tossed over his shoulder, as he headed back to his car. He slammed the door without waiting for a response.

CHAPTER 4

Okay, so I was wrong about this whole coffee shop thing taking off. Unbelievable. A line for coffee. What's next? Coffee drive-thrus?

The smell of coffee hit him as if he had fallen into a pot that had been freshly brewed.

Well, no one's going to notice the chlorine.

Linc pulled all the money from his pocket and looked at the numbers on the bills, but when the hairs on the back of his neck stood at attention, he scanned his surroundings.

Izzie smiled at him from a table on the far side of the lobby. He slid his money back into his pocket as he approached her table.

"What are you doing on my turf?" She feigned annoyance. "I've never seen you in here."

"It's my first time. Coffee, who knew?"

She looked around, waved him closer, and whispered, "Everyone."

"I wonder what else I've missed by being in the pool."

"Every new day is a new opportunity. But let's not tell anyone else about this coffee shop. I see enough of all of you guys at the pool."

"Too late. The guys are on their way." Linc smiled and leaned in to whisper, "Don't worry. It's not our new hangout or anything."

Izzie's shoulders slumped and her head dropped back.

A group standing at the counter moved to a table. Linc pointed to the barista. "My turn."

"Have a good day, Linc."

"Thanks. See you tomorrow."

"Or, take the day off." Linc heard Izzie's words, but stared at her while he processed them.

And not go to the pool? Come on.

A text alert sounded on Linc's phone. He waved at his assistant coach. People looked up from their books as the alert rang out a second time and he fumbled to silence the phone. As he walked toward the counter the chick behind it captured his attention.

Niceeeee. Look at you, little too much make-up, but cute face. Very nice smile.

The vibration in his pocket reminded him of the message. A quick check revealed a text from one of his favorite people, and there was no doubt what the contents of the text would be. A word-of-the-day calendar that Linc had purchased for Grace a couple of Christmases ago had morphed into a word-of-the-day text game for the two siblings.

Grace: Word of the day...ostensible

"Well, hello." A tall blonde with a syrupy voice spilled over the counter toward him. "What can I do to be of service to you today?"

Funny, I don't see any golden arches. How many have you served?

Linc gave a small smile while he concentrated on the menu hoping the 'I'm easy and I'll prove it' commentary would stop. "I'll take a medium coffee with cream and sugar. Please."

"Shelley." The barista pointed to her nametag. "Are you certain that's all you need today? There is so much more on the menu."

"I'm good." Linc glanced at each of his bills before paying for the coffee.

Pair of deuces. Saving this one for you, Becks.

Not able to beat his old roommate since their junior year, he'd been saving the best hands for the next time they met.

Laughter stole Linc's attention. It filled the empty space in the coffee shop. He turned toward the laugh.

And stared. He didn't know if it was the fullness of lips, the joy in her face, or her hair, piled loosely on top of her head, that prevented him from looking away. She was definitely different from any of the other chicks he'd ever dated but she was having the same effect.

He tried to see what book she was reading.

Shelley tapped the counter to capture his attention. "Anything else?"

Linc turned back toward the counter. "Nope. Just the coffee.

Thanks."

A muffled version of Linc's new favorite sound escaped the engrossed reader.

Turning quickly, Linc caught her face light up as she laughed.

That's her. That has to be her. Game on.

Linc pushed his shoulders back and slipped into full swagger mode. Picking up his coffee, he strolled over to speak to her. The closer he got, the more taken with her beauty he became. He leaned over her table. "Hi, I'm Linc. You have a great smile."

An invisible wall of emotionlessness slammed down between them. She no longer possessed the beaming smile that had drawn him across the lobby. This mystery woman's straight posture and flat eyes radiated a lack of interest in what Linc was selling.

Ummm...this is a new reaction. This could be fun.

He tilted his head. "May I join you?"

"Why?" the girl snapped.

"I'd like to say hi."

The door of the coffee shop swung open. Sunlight fell on her face and illuminated the gold flecks in her brown eyes.

Linc recognized the voices without looking from the girl. He took a deep breath.

"My friends are here." He positioned his back to his friends.

She glanced at him with a 'you're wasting my time' face, but not in the pouty way Friendship Circle had the night before. In fact, not like any of the girls who had stared at him.

A quick sip of coffee allowed Linc a glimpse of his friends. They were definitely watching. Refocused on her book, the girl showed no interest in continuing a conversation.

Ummmmm...Dude, you just got a major brush off. Like the ultimate, 'I'm done with you.'

"Nice talking to you..."

Insert your name here.

He waited.

Nothing.

His teammates settled at a table across the coffee shop. They clocked Linc's every move and broke out in laughter as he approached.

"Doing some charity work?" Harrison asked, as Linc grabbed a chair from the next table. Linc glanced at Izzie to find her 'you're disappointing me' face staring back.

That's excellent. Izzie heard, let's hope Pretty didn't catch it.

Linc arranged his seat next to Mikey with a perfect view of the girl. His mind scrambled with what transpired. A feeling of deflation intensified as the mystery girl walked out.

"Harrison, you're a dipshit. What made you think that I'd be interested in Friendship Circle?"

His friend was caught off-guard. "What?"

"The date you set me up on. The dancer or cheerleader chick you set me up with that lives on Friendship Circle. Dumb ass name for a street."

"Shit, now I can't remember her name. Hold on." Harrison stared at the ceiling.

"Doesn't matter." Linc drank his coffee.

"Bro, it's time to get back in the game. Look what happens when we leave you alone. You're chatting up a total fat ass."

Linc waved him off. "She's cool. She's got some serious basketball knowledge."

"I think you're confused. Look at you, man. Tall, fit, chiseled. Mikey, help me," Harrison continued. "That girl looked like she swallowed a few basketballs."

"Not cool, man," Linc snapped, placing his cup on the table.

"Whatever. Get over yourself. Don't make us worry about you. First, you decide not to go on our spring break trip. Then, it sounds like you rejected the newly named 'Friendship Circle.' Lastly, you're chatting up a fat chick. Is there something you'd like to tell your closest friends? Your teammates? Your second family?"

Mikey waved to Shelley. "Do we know her?"

All the guys turned to look at the barista who had offered to pour herself into a coffee cup for Linc's enjoyment. Uninterested, Linc returned his focus to the cup sitting before him.

Mikey leaned back in his chair with a coffee cup in his hand. Always the one to bring his teammates back from the brink of a fight, Mikey had remained the glue of the team since he arrived on the pool deck and ended a battle between ego-filled seniors with jokes about himself.

He was never one to waste the silence of a room like his best friend, Harrison. "Anyone else see the irony in her name being Friendship Circle? Isn't she making her way around our circle?"

"Yeah, you're both ass hats. I'm out."

Linc grabbed his coffee and walked toward the door. Harrison was right on one point. They were some of his closest friends, but at this moment, he was being a shithead. As he headed into the sunlight, his thoughts returned to the mystery girl.

So, why didn't she tell you her name? What the hell's up with the walls going up and not wanting you to sit down?

CHAPTER 5

What is that?
A faint vibration and a muffled ring went off simultaneously.
Dude, it's your phone.
Linc slid his hands under the pillow enwrapping his head.
The vibration and ring went off again.
Linc groaned.
Phone.
He thrashed around the sea of blankets and sheets in search of his phone and finally answered without checking.
"Hello?"
"You're still sleeping?" He smiled, as he mashed his face into the pillow. "Isn't there a pool calling your name?"
The clock by his bed had been turned the night before to hide the annoying blue glow that had been intensified by the beer he had consumed while playing *Halo* with the guys. He knew by the sun seeping around his blinds that he'd slept in.
He pretended to be angry. "Grace, do you have any idea what time it is?"
Linc's sister giggled. Her move to Italy had been an adjustment. Her laugh poked at his heart. Grace knew how much he missed her. Words weren't required, but the phone calls and text increased after the move.
"Like I give a shit what time it is. Wake up and tell me if you've made a decision about coaching or taking the teaching job."
"I haven't decided." Linc sat up and placed a pillow behind his back. "I figured I'd get through my exams and decide during spring break."
"Partying in the Keys isn't really conducive to making life decisions."
As he had on so many calls, Linc listened while Grace moved around the kitchen in her flat. When she initially had moved into

the apartment, noises had been explained as they spoke. In the months of shared calls, Linc figured he knew every corner of her new house.

Grace made no effort to keep the noise down for her brother who had only just arisen. Pots banged together, forcing Linc to move the phone away from his ear.

"You alright over there?" he inquired of his only sister.

The banging stopped abruptly. "Yes."

"Okay."

Duh, I know there's a guy there.

"We're talking about you today, Lincoln."

"Oh, shit. You broke out with my full name. What are you hiding?" Linc asked slowly.

"Mom said you had a date last night. How'd it go?" Grace manipulated the conversation expertly.

And, of course she knew I had a date.

Linc closed his eyes and banged his head against the headboard. "Do I want to know how Mom knew I had a date last night?"

"I could tell you it's because she loves you very much and she wants to be involved in your life. But, I don't want lightning to strike me down where I'm sitting."

Linc nodded. "Right."

"I think she called Harrison to ask about spring break. You can't tell her I told you..."

"Duh! Agreed."

Grace laughed. "She's lining up interviews for you and needed to know the exact dates of the trip."

"Interviews?"

"Perhaps interview isn't the right word. Apparently, she's arranged for you to meet with a couple of representatives to work in their offices over the summer."

He climbed out of bed and began pacing. "Grace, are you shitting me?"

"Herbert? I wouldn't. It gets worse." She hesitated. "Harrison texted her a picture of the girl you went out with. She already has you married off."

Linc fell on the edge of the bed stunned. "I'm not working in a political office. I wish she'd let that go."

Grace laughed. "Good luck with that."

"As for the chick, she was ridiculous."

"Linc, don't be disrespectful. Chick is a shitty thing to call a woman," his sister scolded him.

"Sorry. I don't remember her name so I've been calling her Friendship Circle. FYI, the date was horrible, and she was ridiculous."

The noise on Grace's side increased. His sister was always on the move, so he didn't pay much attention. "Advice?" she offered.

Linc smiled. "Always."

"Tell Mom to cancel the job interviews. Let her mourn the dream of her son becoming a politician. She'll come around. You're her favorite."

"I'm her favorite because you refused to pursue acting, Grace Kelly. Besides, I'm planning on telling her once I've made a decision." Linc flopped back on his bed.

"Fine. Gotta go. What's the word of the day?"

He dragged his hand over his face. He knew he was busted. "It's super early, and I don't have one yet."

She cleared her throat. "What was the word of the day yesterday?"

"Come on, Grace. Seriously, I'm not even awake yet."

"Nugatory. Look it up. Use it. And next time, be prepared," his sister demanded. "Oh, did you get the shirts?"

The open shipping box remained on his desk. "Yes, they fit perfectly. Finally, I have cuffs that reach my wrists. Thank you."

Grace had found a tailor who made custom shirts. This tailor's shirts were different because they fit. Linc's dad hadn't concealed his annoyance at Linc waiting for his sister to move to Italy to share his clothing dilemma.

"Dad told me to order a bunch if you liked the fit."

"Nice. Do you want me to call him?"

"Nah, I'll just order some and take it out of my allowance."

Remembering when Grace tried to tell their dad she didn't need the monthly deposit popped in his head. He chuckled at the way their dad had blown off the notion of her needing to make it on her own.

"I gotta run. Most."

"Most," Linc returned.

Linc knew she disconnected the second she heard him say 'most.' The siblings had started using the word as a replacement for 'I love you the most' when they were in elementary school. It had been Grace's way to make sure Linc knew she loved him without being embarrassed in front of her friends. It had become something the two shared.

He started to set the phone on the bed next to him, but it vibrated in his hand.

Grace: Nugatory. Don't forget!

. . .

The door closed, pushing Linc further inside the coffee shop. The girl who hadn't been far from his thoughts sat alone at the same table she had been last time he had approached her.

Okay. Let's try this again. There's no possible way she's not picking up what you're putting down. Shit, Linc, you sound like an asshole. She's totally going to blow you off again.

Linc lowered his backpack gently to the table. "May I join you?"

"More charity work?"

He flinched at her biting words and sat down across from her. He glanced at her as he dug his book out of his bag.

Daggers. This isn't going to be easy.

After a few seconds, he looked into her eyes and said, "My friends are assholes."

"Well, that speaks volumes about you," she retorted. She returned to the book in front of her.

Her hair was stacked messily on top of her head with loose bits hanging down her bare neck.

How'd I miss those two freckles under your eye?

He noted her lashes were incredibly long and her skin seemed fresh compared to the last woman he sat with.

And, you smell so good. Dude, say something.

"I heard you the other night collecting money from your bet."

Her eyes narrowed. "You're going to need to be a little more specific than that, I'm afraid."

What the hell? Who is this girl? Is she running numbers?

Linc closed his book and leaned forward. "The night after the playoff game in the diner. OT foul shot. 'Padgett is your boy!'"

She laughed, and it sounded like pure happiness and smart-ass twisted into a bow.

That laugh is amazing.

"Easy money," she said, as she continued laughing.

As suddenly as she laughed, she stopped. "What do you want? I need to study. I don't have time for jokes–"

"Great, let's study," he said, cutting her off. He opened his textbook and started reading. He felt her studying him, but bored in on the Principles of Secondary Education.

After an hour, Linc stretched and stood up. Linc's eyes traveled over her face as if she were a live painting. She looked up him, and his heart flopped.

"Would you like a refill?"

"I'm fine."

"Finally, we've found some common ground. But I was asking you what you want to drink."

He watched her expression morph from confusion to embarrassment. Her mouth opened and shut without words escaping.

You could tell me your name.

As Linc approached the counter, Shelley greeted him with a full-teeth smile. "Well, look who came back. What can I get for you today?"

"Do you see the girl over there in the oversize MSU shirt? Do you happen to know what she orders?" Linc turned to catch the girl looking him over. Her eyes quickly returned to her book.

And, there it is. Confidence level back where it belongs.

Annoyed at being ignored, the barista's bubbly disposition faded. "She's a vanilla latte and a coffee cake muffin."

"I'll take two of the latte things." After checking the numbers on a twenty, Linc paid for the coffee. He turned, hoping to catch her eyes on him again.

Come on, Pretty. Show me your eyes.

"I'm going to make yours special," Shelley added with a wink, as she handed him the change.

He leaned against the counter and examined his dollar bills for winning numbers. Shelley winked again as she set the coffees on the counter.

Thanks, but no.

Linc placed one of the cups in front of his tablemate. "One vanilla latte." He settled in across from her with his first ever vanilla latte.

"This one's yours."

Linc smiled at her. "Nope. They're the same."

The girl, whose name remained unknown, slowly turned her cup. A phone number and 'Call Me, Shelley' was written in bold black marker.

Are you shitting me?

The pretty mystery girl's eyes held no emotion. He grabbed the cup and walked purposefully to the counter.

"Excuse me, Shelley." Linc held up the cup with her handwriting. "This is flattering. I guess. But I'm trying to get that girl to go out with me and this is NOT helping. So, would you please pour this coffee into a new cup without your name and phone number so I can have half a chance?"

Shelley glanced at the girl and her mouth opened with a look of shock.

"You're joking."

Linc shook his head. "Afraid not."

Shelley poured the latte into an unmarked cup and placed the coffee on the counter, and then walked through the 'employee only' door without another word.

He placed the latte in front of the girl who was making him work harder than any other girl ever had.

Don't be a pussy! Just ask.

"So, will you go out with me?"

CHAPTER 6

Still can't believe she said no. And, how do you not know her name yet? What the hell? Shit, why did she say no? Why the hell is she still on your mind? Because, dumbass, that smile.

Linc pressed pause on *Call of Duty* to listen for a repeat knock on the door. Hearing it again, he got off the couch. Curious why the visitor wouldn't just walk in, Linc opened the door. Friendship Circle stood smiling back at him.

Quick, close the door!!

"Hello, Linc." Her voice oozed with an overly sultry tone.

"What's up?" he said flatly.

"Can I come in to chill for just a bit?" She took a step to walk in.

"Ahhh–"

"Come on. I don't bite."

What do you want? This is not going happen.

Linc moved back to allow the chick he had wanted to drop kick out of the car just a couple of nights ago to enter. Pointing to the chair adjacent to the sofa, he sat down in his spot again. "Have a seat."

Picking up the controller, Linc started the game. Theme music filled the space.

Ignore her. Maybe she'll leave.

Friendship Circle walked slowly around the sofa and lowered herself next to Linc. Very close. Feeling crowded, he shifted toward the armrest in an attempt to put more space between them.

How the hell does she know where you live? You're dead, Harrison. This chick is jockin' you hard and the one you want to talk to is ignoring the shit out of you. What is she doing here? Damn it...dead, again.

"I don't play video games. Did you just lose?"

Linc turned his head to look at the chick sitting in his personal space and asking dumbass questions. "Yeah."

With a huge smile on her face, she took off in a completely different direction. "I just bought several new bikinis for Key West. I'm positive there's at least one you'll like. Are you looking forward to the trip?" She flipped her hair and moved closer.

He focused on the TV screen as a new game began. "I'm not going."

"Oh. I hadn't heard that," Friendship Circle replied, her voice dripping with disappointment.

"Well, we're even. I didn't know you were going either."

A shrill laugh came out of Friendship Circle and her head fell back. Linc paused the game to look at her.

Is that your laugh? Stop! Just, stop. Okay. You need to get out of here, immediately.

"You're teasing me now."

Linc shook his head, unsure what she was talking about. He mashed down on the play button to restart the game.

"Wait...are you seriously not going to Key West with all of us?"

"I don't know who 'all of us' are, but I'm not going on the trip that most of the swim team is going on."

Friendship Circle sat silent. He thought he heard the wheels turning in her head. "This is a nice room. Can I get a tour of the rest of the house? Maybe your room?"

Linc paused the game and set the controller on the coffee table. He looked over at the chick next to him whose name he didn't care to know. "Look, I'm going to be honest with you. I'm interested in someone else at the moment. So, nothing's going to happen here."

She sat there pouting for a few more minutes. Or maybe scheming. Then, without saying a word, Friendship Circle huffed out the door.

Finally. Why can't Pretty knock at the door to chill? That would be something. Come on, Linc, you need to get her to tell you her name. New plan needed with this one.

The next few hours were lost to *Call of Duty*. It wasn't until Mikey and Harrison walked in that he looked up and realized it was dark.

Mikey knocked Linc's feet off the coffee table and sat in the chair he'd claimed a year earlier when Mrs. James had refurnished the entire house. Harrison walked to the kitchen and returned with three opened beers, handing them out as he took his regular seat on the opposite end of the sofa from Linc.

Mikey started in immediately. "What's up with you and Friendship Circle?"

Linc tossed the controller on the coffee table.

"What's up with her? And what's up with you?" His voice, already riddled with annoyance, slid into anger. "Since when is it cool to tell a crazy person where I live? She dropped by earlier."

He snatched the controller back off the table and restarted the game.

"Tap that. No effort needed."

Linc grimaced and shook his head. "Really not interested."

"I told you, Harrison," Mikey chimed in.

"I question how well you know me with that hook-up."

Mikey raised his beer toward Linc. "Tell him..."

"Yeah, Harrison, tell him!" Linc said stronger.

Harrison leaned forward to grab the second controller. "Friendship Circle, as you so affectionately call her, came to me and asked to be set-up on a blind date. She wanted to go out with you and thought going through one of us would work best."

"When were you going to tell me she was going to Key West?"

Mikey and Harrison looked at each and burst out laughing.

"She has some serious stalker tendencies. She's into you, and it's been awhile for you," Mikey was able to get out between laughter.

"Thanks for your concern for my sex life. Strange. But, no thanks. I'm good."

"Don't be a pussy. You're not 'good' or you'd be chasing ass."

"She's not going to be pleased when she finds out you aren't going on the trip," Mikey tossed out from left field.

Linc smiled, "She wasn't happy. It was priceless."

CHAPTER 7

Wow...could you be more disappointed that she isn't here? She doesn't live here. Grow a pair, would you? Total chick move to sit at her table, and you're doing it.

A voice came from behind the coffee maker. "Alexis won't be here for another hour."

Linc smiled gratefully at the girl who stepped into view.

Alexis.

"I mean, if that's who you're looking for. I heard you talking to Shelley the other day."

"Yep, you nailed it. I'm not only looking for her, I'm looking for any information about her that you might be willing to share."

The barista crossed her arms and tilted her head back. She gave Linc the once over.

"I'm not a murderer or anything."

She held up a finger when a customer walked to the counter. Linc stepped back to wait for her to have a free moment. When she joined him, he continued without allowing her to say a word, "Look..."

She pointed to her nametag. "JoAnne."

"Hello, I'm Linc. JoAnne, I'm having trouble getting her to go out with me. Is she seeing some–"

For real? Another customer?

As JoAnne made coffee, Linc moved to Alexis' table. Flipping a notebook open, he stared blankly at his notes. Customers flowed to the counter non-stop.

Seriously, coffee shops. No one makes coffee at home anymore.

Linc bolted to the counter as the last customer was served. JoAnne was wiping down the machine. He waited for her to drop the cloth.

"JoAnne, I need your help. She's like no one I've ever met. I'd like to get to know her. Help me?"

Shit...fuck...damn. Could you possibly come off more pussy-whipped? You don't even know this girl, Alexis, and you're spilling your guts all over the counter. Jesus.

JoAnne placed her hands on her hips. "This better not be some kind of sick prank because she's a fat girl."

"What? No!"

She leaned on the counter and looked him up and down. "Fine! Alexis studies here a lot. She likes sports."

"And?"

JoAnne looked at Linc for a half a second and frowned. "And what? What did you expect? I don't know you. That's my girl."

He held his hands up. "Touché. Shit, I'm just pumped to know her name."

Customers were still filing into the cafe. Linc moved away from the counter. "Who knew this place did so much business."

"This is our slow time. They're going 24 hours in June," JoAnne declared, as she left him to wait on the new coffee drinkers.

Seeing JoAnne was going to be busy for a while, Linc returned to Alexis' table.

Alexis. Finally! Loves sports. Sport? Basketball? Should've asked the boyfriend question. Nah, she was definitely checking me out. Girls don't check guys out if they're with someone.

Reassured that Alexis was into him, Linc tried to focus on schoolwork, but his concentration waned each time the door opened. The possibility of Alexis walking in kept him on high alert.

Alexis slammed her bag on the table. "What the hell are you doing here?"

Shit! You scared the shit out of me. How'd I miss you?

"Studying?" he replied quietly, lowering the textbook he had become engrossed in.

"Here! Why are you here? At this table. My table." Alexis punctuated every word. She wasn't looking at Linc, but at the table.

He swallowed the witty retort on the tip of his tongue. Something seemed off.

She's upset. Be cool.

Linc leaned forward. In a hushed voice, he asked, "Are you okay? I didn't mean to upset you. I'm sorry. I just–"

"And here you go, two vanilla lattes." JoAnne walked up to the table, holding two huge orange mugs. "Just as you ordered."

"The orange one, I see," Alexis said, as she sat down across from him.

JoAnne shot Linc a wink and threw over her shoulder, "Your favorite color."

Alexis slowly retrieved a notebook covered with butterflies of different sizes and colors from her bag. She opened the notebook and began to write.

"I can move," Linc finally conceded, after a full minute of staring at her. "If you want."

Jesus...she has beautiful eyes. Dude, wherever you put your balls, please go back and get them. This girl is freaked out by the fact that you were at her table.

Alexis glanced up at him. He twirled his tongue over the glacier of whipped cream, and she exhaled. Placing a shiny silver pen on top of her notebook, she leaned back with crossed arms. "What are you trying to prove? Is there a bet or something? Some kind of Carrie movie moment that you and your asshole friends want to play out with a fat girl?"

Linc fought to halt the flinch from her comment. Instead, he countered, "Is this how you treat all the guys that hit on you?"

"Just the ones that typically date Barbies and hang out with guys who refer to me as charity."

Barbies? Great...the charity thing is sticking.

A loud group of girls walked in. Both Alexis and Linc watched them make their way to the counter. Linc stole a quick peek at Alexis as she stared at the girls.

Why the sad face, Pretty?

He tried to find her smile. "Interesting. Have you been asking around about who I date? Last I heard, Barbie was already taken."

"Barbies...it's a type." Alexis stressed each word. She wasn't done with her explanation. "The plastic-perfect, overly made up type. The kind you and your friends prefer to have on your arm on a date."

Linc lifted his cup to take a drink, but paused. "So, you've been asking around about me."

Alexis blew out a huff of air and opened her notebook. She began to write fast and hard.

"Two questions." He took a sip, waiting for Alexis to give him her full attention. When she finally looked up, he continued. "First, what if you're wrong?"

Alexis rolled her eyes as she returned to writing.

Convinced she was listening, Linc pressed on. "Second, what if I am interested in you?"

There you go, Pretty. All the cards on the table.

Alexis sat back in the chair. Her eyes darted from Linc to the people sitting at the tables around them as if there was a chance they were listening. She laid her hand on her chest, and she lowered her head so her chin rested on the top of her hand. A perfect amount of hair fell to hide her eye.

Ha! Speechless.

Then, she grabbed her bag off the chair next to her and marched out the door without another word.

Linc rubbed his hands over his face.

Alexis' butterfly notebook sat on the table in front of him.

You know, this is almost a sign.

JoAnne walked over with a to-go cup as Linc was putting his book into his backpack. Without asking, she transferred the remaining latte into a paper cup. As she placed a lid on securely, she mumbled, "I'm sorry. More fish in the sea. Or something like that."

"What? This was our first date."

Smiling at JoAnne, Linc slid Alexis' notebook into his bag, grabbed the coffee, and walked out the door.

CHAPTER 8

It could be notes for class. Maybe it's all the numbers she's running on campus. Numbers? You're a dumbass. It looks like a journal. Pros...it could give you all kinds of insight into what she's thinking. Bonus, there might be something about a certain handsome swimmer dude that's been hanging around a lot. Cons...total asshole move to invade her deepest private thoughts. Crossing this line could ruin any chance for you to get to know her.

Linc broke the silence in his room. "I could be helping her by reading this."

He reached for the notebook, then stopped and pulled his hand away before making contact with the cover.

"Man, you know better than this. Your sister and your mom wrote in journals. Grace would kick your ass. You can't violate her personal thoughts."

Each butterfly began to mock him.

Your chance could've been blown when you picked this up.

Linc rolled his neck and took his long right arm over the front of his body for a good stretch. He repeated the same movement with his left arm. He had been out of the pool too long. Exam weeks always played havoc with him.

"It might not be a journal."

Linc snatched up the notebook, leaned back in his chair on two legs and flipped to a random page near the front. He stared at Alexis' handwriting. The writing pressed into the paper as if she was forcing the pen to give the paper her thoughts. He hadn't read any words yet. He could still put the book down, but his eyes were drawn to the expletives scrawled across the page.

"FUCK!!! NYC!!! I can't fucking believe I can't fit in the fucking airplane seat. I'm going to miss out on fucking NYC. What a loser. FUCK!!!!"

Linc slammed the journal shut.

Shit!

He tossed it back on the desk. "Definitely a journal. Mental note: never tell her you read it."

Flopping on the bed, he examined the San Francisco poster hanging on the wall across from his bed. Closing his eyes, the words he'd just read ran through his thoughts. How Alexis must have felt when she wrote those words.

The fight song bellowed into the room. Linc reached for his phone. His eyes found the journal on his desk as if it were a beacon.

You shouldn't have read it.

"What the hell? We're leaving in the morning, and you're still at home." Harrison started in without giving him an opportunity to say hello. "Are we hanging out tonight, or are you going to pussy out on that too?"

"Yeah, I'm comin'–"

"Change of plans. The party's coming to your place. We leave too early to deal with the mess, so we nominated your place. Sort of your gift to all of us for skipping out on the vacation."

"Tell him he owes us," Mikey yelled in the background.

"Negative, Ass hats. I have that exam tomorrow," Linc said. "Hence, me not going on the trip. I'm only hanging out for a few hours, then more studying. Let's hit a bar...first round is on me."

"Your friend is being a pussy," Harrison informed Mikey. "Harpers or Beggars?"

"Beggars," both replied in unison.

"I gotta run. Someone's at the door."

Harrison confirmed, "Man, Beggars in an hour!"

"Yep."

Linc pushed the end button as the knocking turned to pounding. He glanced at Alexis' journal as he grabbed his wallet off his nightstand.

"Coming."

As his hand reached for the doorknob, his stomach flip-flopped at the thought that it might be Alexis.

You're kidding. She's trying this again. Unbelievable.

With arched back, her hands on her hips, and a big smile on her face, there stood a chick he had rejected twice. Linc blinked repeated as a wall of perfume came crashing in on him. He watched Friendship Circle's dark purple lips as she spoke. "I hear we're having a going away party here. I came early to give you a hand setting up."

"Ah. Sorry, but you were misinformed. No party tonight." Linc began to close the door. "Have a great evenin–"

"Wait!" She stepped closer.

I'm going to die from this perfume.

"I'm already here. How about a party for two instead?"

"Really? I told you already. I'm into someone else."

"Is she here?"

"No."

"Well, I am. Seems it's your lucky day..." Friendship Circle placed her hand on Linc's arm and slowly dragged it toward his chest.

His flinch didn't stop her from touching him, so Linc grabbed her wrist to remove it from his body.

"Actually, I'm–"

Alexis was walking up the sidewalk in front of the next house.

"Alexis!" Linc brushed past Friendship Circle. "Hey, Alexis. You found me."

Alexis stopped. "You have something of mine. I'd like it back."

"Yeah, it's in here." He gestured toward the door.

"I don't want to interrupt. If you can just get–"

Linc escorted her passed Friendship Circle. He closed the door, shutting out Friendship Circle on the step.

"You aren't interrupting anything. She's misinformed. Have a seat. Can I get you something? Protein drink?"

Alexis remained standing, arms crossed. "I just want my journal."

"Journal?"

Alexis glared at him.

"Fine, but the least you could do is sit for a few minutes. You've come over out of the blue."

Please work. Please work. Please sit.

"Five minutes. Please." Linc gestured to Mikey's seat.

"Why?"

"Because. I'd like to get to know you."

"Why?"

Linc threw up his arms in desperation. "Because both of us said Kentucky was going to 'implode' the other night."

"Fine, water," Alexis stated, as she sat in the chair next to the sofa.

Linc turned on the TV and the PlayStation and handed Alexis the controller. He fist pumped the second he hit the kitchen.

No. No. No.

And this is why you fill the ice trays every single time.

He placed the empty ice trays back in the freezer, then cranked on the water and let it run a few extra minutes to get cold.

Carefully carrying a glass filled to the rim, Linc stopped by his room for the journal. He could hear *Call of Duty* playing in the other room.

Oh yeah, she's awesome.

When Linc returned to the living room, Alexis paused the game to accept the glass of water and her journal.

Linc plopped down on the sofa. "How'd you find me?"

"That's what you want to talk about?" Alexis placed the glass on the table in front of her and flipped through the journal.

"Not really. I'm just curious."

"How much did you read?" she inquired, without looking up.

"Three sentences. I closed it when I realized it was a journal. I thought it was notes for a class or where you put all your bets."

Smooth. So much for not telling her that you read her deep private thoughts. Well done, Ass hat.

"There aren't a lot of Linc's around. It wasn't difficult to narrow down where you were. Plus, I know some people." Alexis hesitated. "I can't believe I left this."

"My sister and mom journal. It's supposed to be a safe space. Why'd you leave so abruptly?"

"That's what you want to talk about?"

Linc tilted his head. "It's closer."

"I was having a really bad day. I was feeling overwhelmed." Her voice dropped to a whisper. "You're overwhelming. I needed a moment."

"Are you overwhelmed now?"

"A little. I didn't expect to be sitting in your living room...talking."

Linc threw his hands in the air. "Why is it so hard for you to get that I want to hang out with you?"

Alexis picked up the glass of water and took a long drink.

The agitation of her water reminded Linc of the end of a good rain when the last of the drops would hit the puddles and stir up the water.

"Are you going to be around for spring break?" The lift at the end of Linc's question betrayed it being a casual question.

Alexis glared at him.

"What?"

Alexis leaned back. "I guess you didn't read my last entry."

Linc shook his head.

"Yes, I'll be here for spring break."

"Me too. I still have an exam tomorrow."

"Oh, shit!" Alexis stood up. "I should get out of here so you can study."

"Thank you! Why do you get it, and my friends simply can't understand? They're celebrating spring break and leaving for the Keys in the morning. They don't get why I don't want a party at my house, or why I can't hang out at Beggars all night."

Alexis drew back in surprise. "You're going to the bar tonight?"

"Yeah, I'll study after."

"Huh." Linc watched Alexis bite down on the left side of her lower lip and scrunch her eyes together.

What the hell?

"What?"

"Nothing, not really my place. They're your friends."

Alexis turned for the door, but Linc stepped in her path and dipped his head so he could look into her eyes.

"You started. You have to finish...it's the rule."

She shrugged her shoulders. "Just, friends are nice, but you're here for an education and securing the best job you can for your future. It's curious that you'd choose to spend critical study time with friends, who are finished with their exams, drinking instead of preparing for yours."

"Hang out with me tomorrow night. We can do whatever you want."

"Why?"

"I want to get to know you."

Come on. Give. Me. One. Chance. Please.

Alexis paused at the door. "The Planetarium. 7 pm. Tomorrow."

"The Planetarium it is," Linc replied. "I'll be there at 6:55."

CHAPTER 9

You should be studying. She was right. You get to see her tomorrow.

"Right?" Asker shouted over the music.

Linc scanned the table to find all eyes on him. "What?"

The guys all cracked up. Two members of the women's swim team walked up to the table.

"Are you guys driving to the airport?" one of them asked the group.

Harrison pulled one of them onto his lap to chat.

She's so cute. I can't believe she finally said yes. The Planetarium. Huh. She was really cool about the journal thing. I can't believe I told her I read it.

Harrison pushed Linc. "Hello?"

"What?"

"I asked if you'd take us to the airport in the morning."

"Apparently, the fact I have an exam tomorrow keeps escaping you." Linc slowly spun the bottle in a small circle.

When he had arrived at the bar, only Mikey and Harrison were at the table. They were already well on their way to getting trashed. Greeted with the familiar name calling, Linc ordered a round of Jagermeister shots for his friends and a Rolling Rock for himself. Over the next hour, more teammates arrived.

"What is up with you tonight?" Mikey asked annoyed.

"Nothing. Tired. I have that exam, and I still need to study."

Not interested in Linc's educational pursuits, Harrison barked, "Man, we're leaving in a few hours. Can you please help us celebrate our departure?"

"You're getting on a plane to Florida, not enlisting in the Marines. Chill the hell out. I said I'd come out for a while. I'm here."

"Something's up?" Frank announced, as he set a bucket of

beers on the center of the table. He grabbed one and stood directly across from Linc.

Everyone turned toward Linc. "Nothing is up. I'm concerned about an exam. I should be home studying. That's it."

"He needs to get laid," Frank concluded.

All the guys busted out laughing. Linc nodded.

Mikey waved down the waitress for another round of Jager. Once she moved from the table, he said, "Harrison tried to hook him up with–"

"For fuck sake! Don't say her name. She'll pop up like a bad penny," Linc implored. "She has come by my house twice this week."

"What's the problem?" Mikey laughed.

"I'm not interested in a chick that everyone's had in their pocket. Especially one willing to jump into mine so easily." Linc looked back at the bottle. "Plus, she's not that interesting."

Alexis studying or Friendship Circle sitting on the sofa? No contest.

"Sometimes, the easy ones are more fun," Asker countered, as he grabbed a shot off the waitress' tray. "I happen to know she's a lot of fun."

The waitress worked her way around the table with the Jager. She placed one in front of Linc, and he quickly moved it in front of Harrison, who wasn't paying attention.

"Sorry about this." Linc apologized for his friends. "Are we always this bad?"

Without hesitation, she replied, "Worse."

Linc recoiled at her honesty. "Can you cash me out, please?"

She nodded and removed herself from the table as fast as possible.

For the first time, Linc sat on the outside of the party and observed his friends interacting. Not just his friends, his teammates, who had never held a grudge against him for losing the championship. The night of the race, the team told Linc 'we win together and we lose together,' but each member told him privately that they knew he blamed himself, and that they forgave him. The guilt was what kept Linc at the bar that night.

The conversation revolved around their upcoming trip. This final spring break trip to Key West had been planned for a year.

Graduation was on the horizon. Everyone realized the party ended after this. Real life required them to go their own way.

So, Alexis said yes. What's with her making you beg for her to go out on a date? That smile. That laugh.

"Here you go." The waitress interrupted Linc's thoughts with the bill.

"Hold on." He glanced at the bill as he pulled out sixty dollars. Linc handed her both the cash and the check. "We're good."

She examined the bill.

"Yeah, for all the times I was an asshole in the past. I'm sorry."

She spread the three bills out and laughed. "You still owe me. But this is a great start. Thanks."

Linc laughed as he watched her walk around the table dealing with his drunk friends. "I'm going to head out. You guys are way too much fun for me tonight."

Shouts of 'come on, stay', 'don't pussy out', 'have another shot with us' came from all different teammates.

"No can do. Time for me to be responsible." Linc stood firm.

Loud boos echoed around the table, and people from the surrounding tables joined in. Linc laughed at all of it. Alexis' words about why he was at college played on repeat.

He leaned into the center of the table. "Hey guys, today's the waitress' birthday, and she's stuck here at work. Tip her in style tonight."

"That sucks!" Mikey said.

Frank added, "Hell yeah."

"Oh, we've got her covered!" Harrison said reassuringly.

"Let's get her shots." Tim chimed in.

Satisfied, Linc waved one last goodbye to his friends. He could hear them starting the first round of 'Happy Birthday' as the door closed. His friends exhibited asshole tendencies at times but, down deep, they all had hearts.

All obligations to his departing friends fulfilled, it was time for Linc to concentrate on the exam keeping him in East Lansing over break. Alexis was correct. This was a critical time and doing well on this exam was necessary.

Linc replayed their conversation on the walk back to his house.

Overwhelmed. She was overwhelmed. I make her nervous. Wait...'I just needed to get away from you at that moment.' That's not a good thing. Chill out, Dude. She's going out with you tomorrow night.

CHAPTER 10

Are you kidding me? What time is it? Are you shitting me?!?
Linc yanked the covers back in a tornado of bedding in search of his phone.

"6:15 pm!"

NO! NO! NO!

In and out of the shower in record time, he blew out the door still buttoning his shirt. As he ran down the street, he determined his car would be a parking liability. Typically, the planetarium was a twenty-minute walk across campus, but he knew he could make it in less.

Linc reached for his phone to text Alexis when he remembered he didn't have her number.

No number. Seriously.

He picked up his pace. As he reached the planetarium, he spied Alexis standing in front of the building wearing a pink top and jeans. She hadn't noticed him, and he watched her pull down the front of her shirt. Then, she tugged on the back.

Linc stopped short to catch his breath and allow Alexis to see him.

"Alexis."

As she turned toward him, she drew in a deep breath. Linc hadn't realized she was tense until he watched the tension in her shoulders and body relax with an exhale.

"I'm sorry. I'm late. I overslept."

He wrapped his long arms around her for a quick hug and felt her body tense. After a moment, he felt an arm come up around the middle of his back in a light return hug.

"I figured you had a late night."

"Yeah, I was up studying almost all night." Linc stepped toward the door and opened it for Alexis to walk through.

"How'd it go?"

"Good. Actually, really good. I think I blew it out of the water." Linc scanned the area for the ticket counter.

"I got the tickets already," Alexis said, holding up two tickets.

"Thanks." Linc took both tickets. "I've got ice cream after, then."

Alexis looked away, smiling.

Linc followed Alexis to one of the displays. "Have you been here before?"

"Of course. Haven't you?"

"Nope. First time." Linc allowed a laugh to escape.

"Really," Alexis said, examining the moon rock display. "That's interesting."

"Why's that?" He looked at the same display, puzzled at her fascination.

"Not many people have access to an actual working planetarium on their campus. We have one of the best in the country, and you've never been. I'm guessing you've never been out to the telescopes either, then."

Linc shook his head and watched Alexis as she continued to examine the displays.

"Is this your major or something?"

Erupting into the same laugh that caught Linc's attention the first time he had heard it, Alexis stopped to clarify. "I'm a business major. I just appreciate all that State has to offer. The planetarium happens to be one of my favorites."

Alexis turned to face Linc. "What's your favorite place on campus?"

"The pool," Linc responded, without giving it a second's thought.

"Why?" Alexis searched his eyes.

Feeling exposed, Linc answered honestly. "I'm on the swim team."

Alexis tilted her head slightly. "Super."

The chimes indicating the star show was starting began to ring throughout the lobby. Alexis motioned for Linc to follow her into the observation room.

Wait...what's SUPER mean? She didn't seem all that impressed with that response. Did I miss something? She asked me my favorite place on campus, and I said the pool.

Linc stared at Alexis for a half second longer.

She's unique.

He stepped into the room a step behind her.

WOW! This is something.

He paused. Surveying the sea of chairs, the design of the room caught Linc off guard. The circular closed-in construction, meant to maximize the visitors' and researchers' experiences, made the room appear boxed in.

Several rows back, Alexis sidestepped in six seats. Linc followed without question.

"Sort of feels like we're in a round box," he said, laughing at his own joke and sitting down next to her.

"This from the guy who spends all his time in a fishbowl."

"Hey, there are outdoor fishbowls," Linc replied, laughing even harder.

"Do you spend much time in the outdoor pool?"

"A lot. It's open from March through October." He answered with the knowledge that no one outside the team would ever understand the life of an MSU swimmer. "Alright, so. How often do you come to the planetarium?"

"I try to catch every show. I've missed a couple."

"Show?"

"When you said you've never been to the planetarium, I thought you meant this one. You've never been to any planetarium?"

"Certified planetarium virgin," he confessed.

Alexis laughed.

Worth it. Although, you're one of the few girls that have actually laughed at me to my face, and you do it quite often.

He turned in his seat to face Alexis. "Alright...alright. Answer my question, giggly girl. It's a good thing I like your laugh."

Alexis swallowed her laughter, but the big smile remained in place.

"We aren't just going to sit here and stare at the stars. There's a star show."

"Star show?"

Alexis nodded.

"So, that's the official name. Star shows."

"Absolutely," Alexis adamantly responded, as she tried to

adjust in the seat next to Linc.

He pressed the button on the chair and pushed the arm back to remove the separation between them. "Yeah, I'm challenging Star shows as the official name, but I am intrigued."

"Okay."

"Alexis."

She inhaled quickly.

Trying to find her eyes seems like a great way to pass the time. One second, she's straightforward and in control. The next, she melts into a puddle when I say her name. Okay, but you're thinking about her melting. Too bad they aren't playing sappy music. Who are you? Chill out, Dude.

"So far, you know I'm on the swim team and will graduate with a degree in education. I know nothing about you other than you're a business major. Oh, and you like vanilla lattes."

Alexis nodded. "They're my favorite."

"And, you know basketball. Rumor has it, all sports."

"Ah, rumor has it."

You know more about her. That was a dumb ass path to take. Think, Man. Think.

"I'm guessing you like butterflies."

Alexis squinted her eyes in question.

"Your notebook."

"That you read."

"That doesn't count, as it has all been forgotten. Tell me something else, please."

"Whatever, you're correct, I'm trying to decide on the perfect butterfly for a tattoo."

Linc drew back stunned.

You don't seem like someone who'd get a tattoo, Pretty. Where would said tattoo be placed? Are there other tats?

"I'm full of surprises." Alexis continued. "I want to climb out of MSU and work for a large company that allows me to advance and travel. So I can go places I've never heard of. I want to go everywhere. I want to see everything. What about you?"

"I've been to several places in the States. I like San Francisco. Most of my friends like San Diego but I found San Fran was the place for me."

"Never been."

"You should go. I can show you around."

"Is that where you want to teach?"

"I want to teach wherever I can coach," Linc shared.

A deep voice overhead began narrating what was in store for the audience.

This place is excellent for exploring the universe of Alexis. Oh, that is something I can use later. Universe of Alexis. Don't. Stop. Dang, she smells good. Really good. Dude, you're a dumbass.

In a blink, the stars were out.

"Sweet."

CHAPTER 11

"Thank you for taking me to the star show." Linc repeated for the third time since the lights had come back on in the planetarium. "It was really cool."

"I'm glad you had fun," Alexis replied, standing with her arms crossed in front of herself and her hands linked together.

"What flavor are you getting?"

Alexis scanned the ice cream shop, paying close attention to the tables and chairs placed strategically for maximum capacity. "Buckeye Bliss."

Linc stepped to the counter and brushed his hand across Alexis back to make sure he didn't knock into her.

His touch caused a full body shiver as if she had been jolted by an electric shock.

Hmmmmm

"We'll take two scoops of Buckeye Blitz." Again, he let his hand fall to middle of her back. This time, it wasn't to get her attention, but to have another chance at that shiver. "Cup or waffle?"

"Cup." Her tone was higher than normal.

"In a cup, please." Linc smiled as he continued to order. "I'll take a scoop of Dantonio Double fudge, Capital City Sundae, and Badger Berry Cheesecake in a cup. Thanks."

An angry screech of metal over tile announced a table opening.

"Quick–grab that table and I'll bring the ice cream."

Alexis eased herself between crowded tables to crisscross the small dairy store. She carefully lifted a chair off the ground before pulling it away from the table. As she sat, she glanced in Linc's direction. He smiled, waiting to meet her glance.

Yep, I'm staring at you.

One of the many students behind the counter put the two cups next to the register. "Anything else?"

"No. Thanks." Linc examined the numbers on his bills as one of the staff rang up the sale. A short redhead wearing the same MSU shirt as all the other employees pushed him out of the way to finish the transaction.

"Will this be all for today?" She added a wink to make sure her offer was loud and clear. It was.

Really? I'm on a date.

"Absolutely," he said directly, leaving little doubt.

"That will be $7.75."

Linc spun both cups around before picking them up.

No number.

He set Alexis' ice cream in front of her and slid a chair closer to her so he could pretend to whisper something top secret in her ear. "I didn't want to call you out in front of the help, but you do know you're able to get two separate flavors with each scoop."

Alexis flashed Linc a smile. "I don't like to mix my flavors. If I'm going to have something, I want to taste it."

Linc's spoon paused midway his mouth. Staring at her, he waited to see if she got it.

Boom.

Laughter exploded out of her.

And, she's got it.

Alexis clarified. "I meant ice cream flavors."

Linc just smiled and ate his ice cream.

Oh, there is a little naughty in this one. She smells so good.

"You smell good." The words flew out of his mouth before he could swallow them.

Well that was a little out of the blue. Smooth.

"Thank you?" She pulled all of her hair over to her right shoulder. Her bare neck captivated Linc.

I want to explore you like they explored the solar system. Dude, that's so creepy. Don't talk. Just eat your ice cream. And, stop watching her eat ice cream. You need counseling.

"It's lotion. I rarely wear perfume."

"Huh."

Huh.

Alexis tilted her head and scrunched up her eyebrows. "You were thinking about something. Share."

BUSTED! Hell no!!

"I thought all girls wore lots of perfume and had tons of shoes."
He watched her laugh.

"Not me. I hate shoe shopping too. Kind of surprised I still have my girl card."

Linc smiled at Alexis. It was good to see her starting to relax.

"I don't mind shopping for shoes." Linc took another bite. "Funny, my sister hates shopping for clothes and shoes."

"What about cologne?"

"Not really. I always smell like a pool. Adding anything just sits on the surface."

Leaning in, Alexis brought her face close to Linc's chest and sniffed.

"I like the smell of chlorine. But, I also like the smell of bleach, Pine Sol, and wet soil, so I'm weird."

And that's her breath on me. Okay, wrists flex, fingers facing diagonally downward, elbows rotate. Nope, not thinking about her getting close. Focus on your palms facing backward as you flick the water toward your feet.

Alexis looked down at the cup of ice cream. "I don't know anything about the swim program."

"No one does outside our circle. MSU is a two-sport school. They allow us to be here to make them appear well-rounded."

Ummmm. Dude. Where did that come from? You can't dog the University. Are you pulling it together? It does not appear as if you are pulling it together.

"Aren't most Big Ten schools two-sport universities?"

Linc continued to share his frustration with the school. "They are, but the money filters down to other sports a little bit more at other schools."

"How do you know?" Her genuine curiosity made him want to continue.

"The pool here is the worst in the Big Ten. It's not the right size, it's in need of repair, and it's been on the list for a renovation for years. Yet, our team is pretty lucky. There are several teams that don't have the facilities to practice on campus, so they book time elsewhere.

"The long-term plan for the football complex is ridiculous. Same with basketball."

Alexis listened.

Linc continued. "Don't get me wrong, I like football and basketball. But the school needs to remember there are a lot of other athletes here."

"Is this beat up on MSU day?"

"Never. I serve at the pleasure of Michigan State University."

"That's better." Alexis smiled.

"How do you know so much about basketball?" Linc asked, changing the subject.

"My dad." Either the words or a thought brought a smile to Alexis' face. "He knows more than anyone I've ever met. We watched sports together growing up. Basketball was my favorite."

"Did you play in school?"

Alexis pushed her spoon into her ice cream. "Me? Seriously? No. I cannot play sports."

Linc shrugged.

"I was too fat to play. Duh."

"For high school sports? There were kids all sizes who swam. I'm positive it's like that in all sports, if they had skill."

"Well, I didn't play. Okay?" She poked at her ice cream.

His hands flew up. "Fine."

Alexis looked around and said, "I wanted to be a sports commentator though."

"Why aren't you in communication, then?"

"It wasn't going to be the right field for me. I didn't fit the mold for that path."

Linc heard the tone in her voice and it made him think of the words from her journal. "I wanted to be a scientist."

"Yeah?"

He ate his last bite while nodding enthusiastically.

Alexis still had half of her ice cream left.

With his spoon in the empty cup, Linc grabbed his phone out of his back pocket and offered it to Alexis.

"This has been fun. I'd like to hang out again. Can I finally get your number?"

Accepting the phone, she entered her number and handed it back.

Linc typed out a text:

I liked the star show. Text me when you get home tonight.

"Okay, here's a fun fact about me. I'm named after presidents."

"I figured."

"HLJ." He tilted he head and raised his eyes brows.

"An H. Huh. Interesting. I wasn't expecting that."

"Herbert Lincoln James."

Alexis playfully pushed Linc's arm. "Nice. I can see why you went with Linc. I'm related to a president." She slowly turned the ice cream cup.

He laughed, "Don't tell my mother."

"Okay."

"Which president?" Linc squinted at Alexis as he stretched his legs out.

"Alexis Kennedy Hewson."

"For sure, never, ever tell my mother."

Alexis laughed. "Ready?"

Linc looked in her bowl. "Do you want to take this home?"

"I'm done. Thanks." Her shoulders rose up to her ears and came forward, rounding her back. The bowl rested between the tips of her fingers.

Linc stood, picked up both bowls, and tossed them in the nearby trash.

"Now we have to hang out," he said, when he returned.

"Really?"

"President's Club."

"There's a club?"

"Now there is."

CHAPTER 12

Two days. I can't believe I made it two days and I'm back at the coffee shop. Waiting for her. Focus. Read.

Linc sat at Alexis' normal table, reading. Lost in the pages of a story he had read several times before, her scent dragged him from the pages. He smiled.

"Looks like my plan worked. I was hoping to see you today."

She glanced at the book as she joined him. "Good plan."

"Michael Phelps." He held it up for her to get a look at the cover. "He's going to change the world of swimming."

Alexis nodded.

"So, how's your spring break going so far?"

"Busy, but good." Alexis pulled out a notebook covered in colorful maps.

Sliding his chair back, Linc stood up. "I'm getting coffee. Can I get you some?"

"You don't have to buy me coffee." Alexis reached into her bag.

Linc waved her off. "I do, though. It's payback for you telling me all about your busy day."

Shelley greeted him with a voice so syrupy it would send the creeps down most peoples' spines. "How can I help you today?"

"Two vanilla lattes. Hold the phone number."

Shelley's mouth fell open at being called out.

"Can you add two cookies to that? Chocolate chip and..." Linc turned toward the table, "Hey, Pretty. What kind of cookie do you want? I'm getting chocolate chip."

Alexis snapped her head up in a double take, and her eyes grew round. Linc enjoyed the blush that came over her face.

Alexis pushed out, "Same."

Had the coffee shop been its normal level of busy, she wouldn't have been heard. Linc winked at her.

"Make it two chocolate chip, please." Linc handed over a twenty after inspecting for numbers.

JoAnne walked up behind Shelley and ripped the printed ticket off the machine, "Good afternoon, Linc. How are you and Alexis today?"

"Excellent. Thanks. And how are you?" Shelley rolled her eyes as Linc cheerfully conversed with the inquisitive barista.

"Working spring break. Other than that, I'm good. I can bring this out to your table," JoAnne offered, with a smile.

"Thanks. Appreciate it."

Linc paused as he made his way to the table, long enough to watch Alexis writing in her notebook.

Man, her hair looks so cute all gathered up on top like that. That neck though.

"JoAnne is bringing them over."

"I've been a loyal customer for I don't know–forever. Never had coffee delivered to the table. It's like you're royalty."

"You should go by Kennedy. See if it makes a difference," Linc advised, laughing.

"Because people care that I'm a Kennedy in the most distant, I-don't-get-invites-to-the-compound kind of way."

"How are you related? If you're allowed to talk about it."

Alexis tilted her head to the side. "Allowed?"

JoAnne set on the table between them two large cups and a plate with two cookies.

"Hey, JoAnne. I'm calling bullshit on never getting table service before."

"What about that one time when–"

"Uh, no. Never. Not one single time," Alexis asserted.

JoAnne shrugged her shoulders and tried a different approach. "How about I owe you a free coffee."

"All is forgiven, my friend," Alexis said ebulliently. "How's life with you?"

"It'll be better in about fifteen minutes," she whispered, looking back toward the counter.

"You're alone tonight?"

"Rachel's coming in later." JoAnne pointed out. "But, if it stays this slow, one of us is leaving early."

"Well, come over and talk to us when you get a few minutes.

We'll be here for a while." Alexis raised her eyebrows in askance at Linc.

"Yep," he replied, stuffing the second half of a cookie into his mouth.

A customer entered, drawing JoAnne away to the counter.

Linc swallowed the bite of cookie. "She's really cool."

"Yeah, JoAnne's been kind to me since day one. She works really hard, too. I can't believe she's not in school here." Surprise filled Linc's face, so Alexis explained. "She works two jobs and takes classes at the community college. She's supposed to be at MSU. I'm not really sure what the entire story is, but I know it has to do with her dad being a major drinker."

"Shit, that sucks," Linc mumbled. They sat quietly until Linc broke in. "So, not to change the subject, but I'm changing the subject."

"Okay."

"I'd like to hear about your busy day. Was it a good one?"

Alexis broke off a small piece of her cookie. "Napkins. I'll–"

"I got 'em." Linc leaped out of his chair and returned before Alexis finished chewing the bite of cookie.

She covered her mouth as she chewed. "I was preparing for my trip."

"Trip?"

Alexis broke an even smaller piece off the cookie and slipped it into her mouth. "I've been invited to visit a Chicago firm and interview with them for a position for a possible summer internship."

Wait...What? Leaving?

"Oh. Wow. When do you leave? Is this a firm you'd like to work for?"

Nodding, she sipped her coffee. "I take the train out in the morning. It would be a great place to intern. I don't know if I would stay much after that. The offer came out of left field. I didn't think I was in the running. I just got the email a couple of days ago."

"When you get back, can I take you out for dinner to celebrate?"

Smooth. Real subtle way to see how long she'll be gone.

"I won't know if I got it that quickly."

"We can celebrate you going to Chicago and completely blowing them away." He tried to be encouraging, but really, he wanted to block her from leaving.

"Honestly? I'm really nervous. It's my first time in Chicago." An undercurrent of hesitation laced in her voice. "I wasn't really prepared to go on a last minute interview out of state."

"Maybe that's on purpose. The firm wants to see who steps up in the situation and who doesn't. Some people are only good when they have time to prepare." Linc's gaze bounced from Alexis to the cookie. "Are you going to eat that, or just pick at it?"

"Ummmm."

Linc broke the remaining cookie in half and popped it in his mouth. "What would you have done differently for the interview if you had more notice?"

Alexis peered out the window, as she contemplated his question. She wrapped her hand around her neck and slowly slid it to her collarbone where it stayed.

Dude, did she bust you staring at her neck? You have got to chill. Eyes on her eyes. Good God, her hair is one pull from falling over her shoulders. Seriously, Linc. Be a friend, you dipshit.

"I would've left a day earlier to make sure I knew where I was going. I would've shopped for a new interview outfit. And, I would've done more than just basic research on the company. Oh, and prepared in-depth questions to ask at the interview."

Yes, I can fix this.

"Let's attack your list. Do you have the address of the company? We need to get you from the train station to their office and back, right?"

"It's a two-day process. I'm being put up in a hotel, too." Alexis scrunched her face up like she smelled something awful.

Ask her if she wants you to go and help. Are you freaking kidding me? Although, time on the train together and at the hotel would be fantastic. Too soon. Is it? Dude, you're bordering on Friendship Circle behavior.

"What time does the train leave? Do you want help picking out a new outfit?"

"NO!" she snorted.

"Fine. Next, I've got a buddy in Chicago. He owes me big time. I'll call him, have him meet you at the train, and get you to the company," Linc offered, as he pulled out his phone.

Alexis shook her head. "That's a lot to ask from someone who doesn't know me."

Linc wasn't willing to concede so easily on this one. "He knows me. I helped him out a while back. Let me at least try to call him."

"Thank you very much for the offer. I really do appreciate it. But I don't think it would be appropriate."

"How 'bout I text him for advice on getting you around the city?" He started typing, ignoring Alexis' objections.

> Linc: Hey Shithead, I need your help. My girl has an interview in Chicago tomorrow and doesn't know the city. She is coming in by train. Can you help?
>
> Becks: Your GIRL? I thought you were gay.
>
> L: You wish I was gay, Dude. How are you doing?
>
> B: I'm great. Unfortunately, I am in San Antonio this week on business but shoot me the address. I'll make sure she's taken care of.
>
> L: Thanks. She's nervous as hell.
>
> B: Why aren't you rollin with her?
>
> L: Long story.
>
> B: LOL It always is. Yeah, text me the addy and give her my number so she can contact me. Tomorrow is the vendor show so I will be available.
>
> L: Thanks, Becks.
>
> B: Anytime. What's up with you having a girl?
>
> L: I'm working on making that happen as we speak.
>
> B: I'm out.

"He's in Texas. He wants me to text him the address, but he's got a plan all worked out."

"He doesn't have–"

Linc continued, "He also said to give you his number. He'll be available to make sure you have help if anything pops up."

A follow-up text with Alexis's number left his phone. A second text with the company's address from the handwritten note Alexis had placed in front of him followed. Seeing the hotel name listed, Linc informed his friend 'his girl' would need to get to her hotel, too.

"You didn't have to—"
"I wanted to," Linc said.
"Thank you. I really appreciate it. A lot."
And there's that smile.

CHAPTER 13

Linc: Good morning, Pretty.

Alexis: Uhhh...This is Alexis.

Ummm. I know who this is. You are so cute.

L: Can I give you a ride to the train station?

A: I'm already here. Being early comforts me.

Of course you are.

L: Good to know. Are you feeling better today?

A: Not at all. Now I'm scared.

L: Did you come up with a few questions to ask?

A: Sort of. Not sure how good they are.

L: They're perfect.

A: Thanks.

L: Are you going to let me take you out for dinner tomorrow to celebrate?

Linc waited for a reply. It didn't come.

Come on, man. Relax. She isn't going to escape by train.

He tossed his phone on the couch and turned on the TV. A game was the distraction he needed to deal with Alexis' lack of response.

The text alert sounded just as Linc moved to a new level. Pausing the game, he slowly picked up the phone.

A: Yes.

YES!

L: Cool. Are you on the train now?

A: Yeah, we're departing now.

I should've gone with you, Pretty.

L: Are you going to try to sleep?

A: Are you joking? I won't be able to sleep until I'm back

in my bed.

L: ?

A: I have an interview...remember? Plus, I don't sleep well in strange places.

Noted. Dude, don't be a douche.

L: LOL - Good to know.

A: Smile

Smile? What's smile?

L: Smile?

A: Yeah, it's something my friend from home and I used to do when texting. It means you made me smile with your comment. OMG...nevermind.

Linc laughed out loud.

She couldn't be cuter.

L: Not going to let this one go so easily. I like it. SMILING

A: LOL

L: You should send me a picture of you from the train with that smile of yours.

You're kind of pushing her openness today.

Linc held the phone waiting for a reply with a picture. There was no reply.

All the unrequested pictures you've deleted, and the first time you ask for one, there's no response. Karma.

L: Hello. Did you disappear?

A: I'm here.

He gritted his teeth as he typed the next question.

L: So, was asking for a picture too much?

A: Why?

Ahhhhh...why, what?

L: Why did I ask for a picture?

A: Nodding.

L: I really like the extra insight...smiling.

Linc waited a minute to see if she would respond. She didn't, so he answered her question head on.

L: Alexis, I asked for a picture because I want to see

your smile.

This time, several minutes ticked by without a reply. Linc snapped a selfie and sent it. Convinced the request was too much, he made his way into the kitchen and popped a couple of bagels into the toaster. He stood at the counter with the orange juice carton tipped up as if it were late at night and getting a glass was a ridiculous notion.

Why'd you have to ask for a picture? You couldn't settle for a convo she was giving up freely. Dipshit.

A faint chime rang out. Linc stubbed his toe on the counter and banged his knee on the end table rushing for his phone.

What the hell?

Linc stared at the image. He squinted and tilted his head to see the image in the best light.

Clearly, you are not a professional selfie taker. How does one take such a blurry picture? And why is she completely cut off? Not what I was looking for, Pretty.

Linc smiled.

> L: So, we're going to need to work on selfies.
>
> A: LOL
>
> L: Did the train pop off the tracks when you hit the button?
>
> A: Shhhh. Don't make me laugh. People are already looking at me for taking a picture of myself.
>
> L: Pretty, that was a drive-by selfie attempt. I didn't know phones could take blurry pictures like this.
>
> A: Laughing out loud NOW! People are staring.
>
> L: I'm not getting a new picture am I?
>
> A: I don't think so.
>
> L: LOL...Everyone takes selfies, but ok.

The smell of toasted bagel motivated Linc to go to the kitchen. In the time it took to properly cover two bagels in loads of ham and cream cheese as well pour a tall glass of orange juice, Alexis sent two more texts.

> A: May I ask a question?
>
> A: You don't have to answer.
>
> L: I'm an open book.

Linc took a huge bite of the first bagel and rubbed his hands together.

>L: Ask me anything.

>A: Why do you look at your money so closely before you pay?

Not exactly the probing question I was expecting.

>L: I play Liar's Poker with friends. Serial numbers on the bills are poker hands.

>A: Nodding.

>L: Anything else you want to know?

>A: At the moment, that's all. Thanks.

Linc sat back and finished his bagels.

What are you missing? Screw it, call dad.

Scrolling through his contacts, Linc typed out a text.

>L: Do you have time to talk today?

Knowing the response, Linc walked out to the front porch and sat on the top step.

He smiled when his father's face flashed across the phone in time with an old fashion ringtone. "Hi, Dad."

"What kind of question is 'do I have time to talk to you today?' When have I not had time for you or your sister?"

Though Linc knew, hearing it made him feel less like an interruption. "Just making sure you weren't in a meeting."

"I was. They'll wait. What do you want to talk about?"

"How's Mom?" Linc silently slapped himself on the forehead for starting with that question.

"That bad, huh?" Linc pictured his father sitting back in his big leather chair. "What's going on, son?"

"Dad, I probably should have talked to you about this before, but I didn't know how Mom would react." Linc paused for his dad to say something. Silence. "I skipped the spring break trip to Florida. I had an exam."

His dad listened quietly.

"I have two interviews coming up for high school teaching positions with swim coach responsibilities. I've also been offered an assistant coach position here at State."

"Your mother has it in her head that you should be a

politician."

"I know."

"Sounds like you have some decisions to make." Someone in his dad's office began to speak, but was cut off abruptly.

Linc imagined his father throwing up his hand and whirling his fingers around in a silent order to leave. For as far back as he remembered, his dad had worked long hours and often traveled for business. Grace and Linc had struggled with the minimal time their dad spent at home in his office. Each tried pushing their luck at entering the off-limits room to win coveted attention.

Oh, he just gave someone the hand.

As they got older, the trade-off between his absences and the family's fortune became clear. In time, both learned to ask their dad for time when it was needed. The James family didn't have family days or go on vacations together, but the world stopped whenever they called.

To let the man, who over the years had walked out of deal-making meetings to listen to his son share news of races he'd won, off the hook, he said, "Okay, I gotta get going."

"Son, is there something else?"

"I...I'm not ready to discuss h–"

Mr. James laughed. "I'll be here when you're ready to talk about her."

Linc heard the squeal of his leather chair as his dad stood up. "Call your Mother. She talked about visiting so..."

Linc nodded.

"Lincoln." Linc perked up, hearing his dad use his full name. "I think you'd make a fantastic teacher."

"Thanks, Dad."

"Do you need anything? Money?"

Every call ended the same way.

No need to check his account, the amount that was added monthly far exceeded what Linc ever needed. When the first month's deposit occurred Linc's freshmen year, a call was made to remind both parents. Food and lodging were included in the dorm fees. Every year, the monthly deposit increased without explanation. Grace predicted it was guilt money for never being around and leaving them with their mother.

"I'm good. Thanks. Talk soon."

The phone was already away from his father's mouth when he said, "Call anytime."

Love you, Dad.

Looking at the time on his phone, Linc calculated where Alexis' train should be and sent her a quick text.

> Link: How's it going?
>
> Alexis: Fine. Just reviewing my notes about the company.
>
> L: Nervous?
>
> A: Incredibly.
>
> L: I have an idea.

Linc walked back into his house while he waited for an incoming text. When it didn't come after a few minutes, he continued.

> L: What if you go into your Chicago experience as Kennedy instead of Alexis?
>
> A: Confused.
>
> L: Alexis is nervous about the interview, right? What if from the moment you step off the train you become Kennedy. Not the family but sort of.
>
> A: Become Kennedy?
>
> L: Leave nervous Alexis on the train. Walk in confident and ready, have them call you Kennedy.

You think on that suggestion. I will be right here—

> A: That is an amazing idea. I'm doing it. Thank you!!
>
> L: Cool.
>
> A: Thank you for keeping me company on my trip. Smiling
>
> L: You have Becks' number right? He knows you may call and he is ready to help.
>
> A: I have it. Thank you for that as well.
>
> L: Good luck, Alexis. I'll be thinking about you.
>
> A: Kennedy! I'll text you when I get back.
>
> L: Ok, I'm here if you want to talk tonight after your interview.

Linc hesitated before hitting send.

> A: Nodding

Not waiting until tomorrow to see how this interview goes. She is going to be alone in a hotel tonight. I really should have asked to go with her. Easy there big guy, she just gave you her number.

CHAPTER 14

Linc reads Becks' text for a third time.

    Becks: He's got her.

She's either okay or pissed.

He leaned his head back against the back of the couch and closed his eyes. Thoughts of her leaving surfaced.

Dude, it's only for the summer. Chill out, Man.

A text alert chimed and Linc lifted his phone off his chest.

    Alexis: A car?

    Linc: You made it.

    A: I wasn't expecting a car.

Come on, is there anything about me that is expected?

Linc's laugh echoed in his quite empty living room.

    L: Smiling?

Not willing to be disappointed, quickly laying the cards on the table felt like the best course of action.

    L: Forgiveness works better than permission. Becks suggested, I jumped.

    A: This is so nice. Thank you. Shock.

The tension he held in every muscle released.

    L: LOL

    A: Thank you for the Kennedy suggestion. I think I'm taking you up on it.

Linc fist pumped and gave a loud 'yes' that could be heard over the paused but singing video game.

    A: I will text you when I get to the hotel.

Nice. Waiting until you came back was going to suck.

Linc nodded his head in excitement as he constructed another text.

Dude, relax. You're acting all twelve-year-old girl again.

> L: Let the driver take you around Chicago. The more
> time he spends with you in his car, the more credit he
> gets for the weekend.
>
> A: Pressure.
>
> L: LOL Think of it as charity.

Yikes. Not the best choice of words.

He checked the time to see how many minutes had passed, it felt like forever.

Okay, so only two minutes. Say something.

Alexis' message popped up:

> A: Gotta go, just pulled up.

Linc tossed his phone beside him on sofa. He needed a distraction while Alexis was in the interview, and there was one place he could go to block out the world.

He headed to the pool.

He hadn't taken three steps from his swim locker when the sound of church bells drove him to retrieve his phone.

Thanks, Dad. I would've called her.

Missed call was displayed, but Linc didn't need to unlock the screen to know who had called.

Years ago, Grace and Linc had been blown away when their dad had returned from one of his many business trips with Blackberries for each of them. The two had spent the entire weekend setting up their new devices. Grace was playing with ringtones when the daunting church bell chime rang out. In unison, the siblings had declared it was perfect for Mom.

When Linc received his Blackberry upgrade, the first change he made was his mother's ringtone. His sister had visited him the following weekend with her upgrade in hand, and they had laughed when they discovered Grace had made the same change.

"Lincoln, you told your dad you were going to call me."

"Hi, Mom." Linc's tone was whiny, something he and his sister tended to do when they knew their mother was about to start in on something or give one of those 'you are perfection but' compliments that only a mother can give. "I'm at the pool. I was going to call you after I ate."

As usual, she disregarded all of Linc's words. "Do not use that tone with me."

Linc stood in the middle of an empty locker room knowing he was in for more than he wanted to deal with at the moment.

"A teacher? How could you even think about setting up interviews without discussing it with us first?"

Way to push me in front of the train, Dad.

"Mom, I'm about to get in the pool. Can't we do this later?"

"Herbert Lincoln James! Do not dismiss me."

"I'm not. I just thought I could get my swim in and grab something to eat. You know how hungry I am after."

"Fine. We put some money in your account today because your dad said you didn't really answer him when he asked. You can ask for help if you run short during the month."

"I told him I was good. It's spring break so I'm not doing much–"

Shit!

"Why don't you come home? You know you can swim at the club. We can get you some summer clothes. You're going to need a suit for graduation."

"I can't, Mom. I have to study for an exam on Monday, and I'm definitely not wearing a suit for graduation."

"You can study here. You'll have your entire floor. Grace isn't here."

"I'm staying here this week. I have stuff to do."

"All your friends are in Florida. This is a perfect time for you to come home."

"Mom, Coach is calling. I have to go."

"I doubt it, but I get the message. Bye, Lincoln."

"Bye, Mom. I'll call you this weekend."

"Before then–"

Linc disconnected the call. Seeing several text messages waiting, he sat on the bench in front of his locker.

> Becks: She's been dropped off at the firm. Seth has her bag and is planning on taking her to the hotel when she is ready. Sucks I'm not in town to meet her. How long have you been kickin' it?"

Nice! Becks, you have come through in a big way.

> L: Thanks, man. I really appreciate your help. I'm still working out all the details on that.

The second message was from an unknown number. Linc

rolled his eyes after opening it. Friendship Circle, in a tiny blue bikini, was staring back at him. The caption under the photo read, "Wish you were here so we could have some fun in the sun."

Seriously, now this chick has my number? And delete. Move on!

The third text message made Linc smile. Grace had changed her name to "Sister of the Year" on Linc's phone, and it always made his day when she texted him.

> Grace: Mom is spiraling about your interviews. I'd call her quick or she'll visit. WTD...comportment.
>
> L: Talked to her. Getting in the pool. WTD...vaunting.

As Linc hit the deck, the stillness of the empty pool threatened to derail all of his efforts of keeping thoughts of Alexis at bay. To his surprise, Izzie sat at the far end of the pool deck. He wandered over to talk to his favorite assistant coach. An equally surprised expression flashed across Izzie's face when she glanced up and saw him approach.

"Hey, stranger, I thought you guys already left for Florida."

He slipped his phone under the towel he had grabbed on his way out of the locker room.

"I couldn't go. I had a late exam." Izzie crossed her arms clearly unsatisfied with his explanation. "I needed some time to prep for the interviews."

Izzie smiled. "You made a decision."

Linc put his cap on as he stepped on the starter block closest to Izzie.

I wish.

He stared down at the water as if the answers could be found on the waves. "Nope."

"Even an empty pool makes waves." Izzie was famous for saying shit that made no sense to Linc, but seemed profound. "Did you make that list like I suggested? Pros and cons."

Without waiting for a response, Izzie returned to the catalogs on her lap, which left Linc alone with his thoughts.

"I told my dad." Linc laughed, more to himself than because of the humor of it all. "Who immediately told my mother."

Izzie looked up and waited for the rest of the story.

Unable to wait any longer for the comfort of the water, Linc slid his goggles into place and dove in. Experience had taught him that Izzie wouldn't press for more information than he was willing to give, and true to form, she was quietly waiting when he returned from his first lap. "He said I'd make a great teacher."

Linc treaded water at the side of the pool. A sense of normalcy from being in the pool relaxed his muscles. His body knew it would be pushed once he started swimming, but there was freedom in the predictability of the workout.

Izzie still silently waited.

"My mother...not as supportive."

Izzie nodded. They both turned when a maintenance worker walked through the visitor's entrance at the top of the bleachers. The volume of the phone conversation he was having made Linc think he thought the pool area would be vacant.

"I'm still not sure," Linc continued, raising his goggles to the top of his head.

Izzie stared out over the pool. "This is a decision you'll have to make on your own. Everyone will have an opinion and most will have an agenda. Parents aren't any different. But they tend to have your best interests in mind.

"There will be different chapters in your life, Linc. Whichever direction you decide, step surely and never question your choices. You have a great opportunity here at Michigan State and you have the ability to work closely with kids and make a real difference. Whichever you choose, you cannot lose. Think about how you want to spend your days and nights, the decision will become clear."

Izzie gave Linc a quick wink and a smile before gathering her work and leaving him alone to swim.

CHAPTER 15

Linc flipped through his mail as he headed toward the kitchen. A letter with the blue logo in the corner and the San Francisco postmark stopped him in his tracks. He stared at the logo for another second before ripping it open.

No Shit!

Linc laid the letter on the counter to snap a picture and add a caption.

> Linc: GK, this makes it even more confusing.
>
> Grace: You got it!!! OMG...I'm so proud of you!! Are you sooooooooo excited?
>
> L: I still haven't decided.

His phone rang immediately.

"This is the city you've been wanting to live in since forever. What?" Grace's voice was raspy from sleep.

Shit, she was asleep. Fucking time difference.

"Grace, I didn't check the time. Go back to sleep."

He heard his sister moving around, "Shut up. This is huge! What's to think about?"

"I could stay here and coach. I'd still be around the pool every day...all day. Plus, it's all the way across the country."

"Am I missing something? You knew it was across the country when you applied. You've talked about this city since we visited. Don't bullshit a bullshitter."

Linc didn't say anything.

"What?"

"I don't know if I'm ready to go."

"Please, elucidate me. The word of the day, by the way."

Alexis. I'd be leaving Alexis. Hello, she is interviewing in Chicago. She is interviewing for a summer internship. She'll be back. Get a grip. You've had one date.

"There are just opportunities in this area. I still have the other two interviews and..." Linc's voice tapered off.

"It's your life and I'll always support you, whatever decisions you make, unless they're stupid. I'll completely interfere if you're making a mistake."

"Thanks, Grace Kelly."

"Anytime, Herbert."

"You suck."

"You started it."

"Can I tell you something? Just between you and me."

"If I was there I'd cut you! I keep everything we talk about between us. Tell me."

Linc hesitated. "I met someone. Sort of."

The sounds of dishes clattering and a faucet running rang in Linc's ear. "I need water. How could you not open with 'I met someone?' Proceed."

Linc's stomach rumbled, reminding him why he was still standing in the kitchen. He grabbed a bottle of water and a pack of sliced turkey from the fridge and walked back to the living room. "She barely speaks to me. She wouldn't even tell me her name or give me her number for days."

"I love her already. Keep going." In the time it took to swallow two bites, Grace grew impatient. "Talk!"

He coughed and laughed at the same time. "Chill, I just got out of the pool. I need to eat."

"You need to freaking start talking. Do you know what time it is over here?"

Reminded that he had woken her up, and she probably had a busy day later, he put the turkey back in the package and tossed it on the coffee table.

"Alexis. Her name is Alexis."

"Very nice."

"GK, she isn't like any girl I've ever met. She knows basketball better than I do—"

"And you have extensive basketball knowledge?"

This was the first time he talked to his sister about a girl. Linc considered what he wanted to share. "She doesn't just—"

Grace took over. "Fall for your bullshit?"

Linc nodded. He sat in his silent house.

"Mom's going to be so excited when you tell her."

Linc cringed.

"Don't do it until you are ready for a visit. Trust!"

Closing his eyes, Linc exhaled. "Alexis isn't what Mom would consider girlfriend material."

"This just got interesting. Is she poor, black, liberal, or ugly?"

A scared little laughter escaped Linc. "Actually, not sure if she's a Democrat. I don't know the right way to say this."

"Just say it!"

"Okay...Alexis is big. Wider than most chicks I've dated." The harsh intake of air mixed with a hiss coming through the phone told Linc he hadn't said it correctly. "You told me just to say it. Don't judge."

"A. Fuck you for thinking I'd judge. B. Fuck you for referring to women as 'chicks'. C. You're almost forgiven for not just saying the woman is fat."

Linc smiled. These moments reinforced just how absolutely cool his sister really was. Grace was, by far, one of his favorite people. He missed having her closer.

"Send me her picture. Let me see this Alexis of yours," Grace said. "Why'd you roll your eyes?"

"It's like you have my house under surveillance. How'd you know I rolled my eyes?" Linc laughed.

He thought about how to explain Alexis' lack of selfie skills without making Grace think he was making the shit up. "Grace, she cannot take a selfie. I've never seen anything like it."

Grace yawned loudly. "Well, genius, take a picture of her."

I miss you, Grace.

"I miss you so much. I don't know what I'm doing with Alexis, but I can't stop thinking about her,"

"HL, my advice to you is to talk to her. If you like her, and it sounds like you do, take it slow. Allow her time to feel comfortable with you."

"So..."

"Be her friend first. I need sleep. I love you. And, Linc? I'm so proud of you."

Remembering one last thing to share with his sister, Linc slipped in, "She's a Kennedy."

"What?"

"Not one of the compound kids. But distantly related."

She giggled softly. "Mom is going to pee herself when she finds out."

"Alexis doesn't think it's a big deal. She doesn't really talk about it."

"If Mom finds out she's a Kennedy...you'll be picking out an engagement ring. Democrat or not."

"No kidding. Let's not tell her. Goodnight, Sis. Most."

"Ditto."

Linc picked up the letter and the turkey as he placed his phone on the coffee table. He ate while he reread the letter.

High school math teacher in Oakland, CA. Small swim team with a lot of potential. Starts at the end of August. California. Teaching and coaching. Working with kids, I'd still be on the pool deck. Competitive swimming is over for you anyway.

Linc closed his eyes and pushed all thoughts of his future from his mind.

Alexis. Dinner with Alexis. Time to explore what's going on in your head.

...

The beep and vibration of an incoming text message jolted Linc from sleep. He rubbed his face in the dark living room.

Two missed calls and five text messages. Shit.

> Alexis: Hi. I survived the first part of the interview.
>
> A: I'm on my way to the hotel. Still cannot believe you arranged a car for me.
>
> A: I'm in the room. It's amazing. Like HUGE. Literally, it is the most beautiful room I've ever been in.
>
> A: Hope everything is ok.

Awe, she is concerned.

Linc typed a message back to Alexis.

> L: I just woke up. I'm rather glad you survived as I'm looking forward to our date tomorrow. How'd it go?

While he waited for her reply, he played the voice messages. Drunk friends yelling and laughing into the phone filled both messages.

Delete.

A new text message arrived.

> A: It went pretty well. I feel like I answered the questions thoroughly. I talked to so many people.

> A: Sounds like you did great."

A text with an image came through. A white king-size bed centered between two side tables. Everything in the room was white. The caption read, 'I could live here.'

> L: Nice.

> A: Nice?!? This room is magnificent. I'm not capturing its true beauty in the picture. Giddy

> L: How about you capture some of your beauty? Send me a picture.

Linc turned on the light to snap a couple of pictures of himself laying on the couch. He sent the first and deleted both.

Another image came through.

There you are, Pretty. Very nice!!

> L: Is this from the back of the car?

> A: Yes.

> L: You look great. Thank you for the picture.

> A: Sure.

> L: What are your plans for the night?

> A: Plans?

> A: Confused.

> L: You're in Chicago.

> A: Laughing out loud! Watching a movie on this big TV.

> L: You can do that here. You should be out on the town.

> A: I don't know anyone. Plus, I have to be back over there by 9am.

> L: You know the driver. Call him. I'm sure he'd show you around.

He better keep his hands to himself though. Wait. Stay in the hotel after all. You don't need to meet someone while you are there. Come on, man. Chill out. Stop acting like a twelve-year-old girl.

> A: Nah. I don't want this room to be wasted.

> L: We'd be going out if I was there.

Or would we?

Linc pulled up the selfie to take a closer look. Grinning, he waited for Alexis to respond.

A: Too bad you couldn't come.

Linc's mouth dropped open. He reread the text.

Did she just say that? Is she? Did she just? Calm down. Be her friend first!!

L: Next time. We'll have a blast.

A: Smile.

L: What are you doing in your room now?

A: Filling up the biggest bathtub I've ever seen.

Ummmmm...let's practice selfies now.

L: Bubbles?

A: Heaps. I think I used too much stuff.

L: Is your phone in a waterproof case? Selfie time.

Linc deleted the text before hitting send.

That's not being a friend.

L: Don't get your phone wet.

A: Hold on.

L: Ok

Linc dropped his head back as he hit send.

I should be there right now.

A: Thank you for today.

L: My pleasure. Becks got the car.

Linc turned on the TV to start a game.

A: I mean the texting today too. Felt like you've been around all day. It helped.

L: It's been fun. Thanks for finally giving me your number.

A: I'm going to take a bath.

L: I'm going to imagine you taking a bath.

Linc paused over the send button to reread his text.

Send.

That will give her something to think about. Lucky, I didn't ask for a selfie of you in the bath. This may be pushing.

Minutes went by and no reply. Linc purposefully got lost in his game.

Okay. Stop thinking about her in the bath. With bubbles. With lots and lots of bubbles. Be a friend.

CHAPTER 16

Linc: Good morning, Pretty. Good luck on day two.

Alexis: Thanks. You're up early.

L: This is late for me. Pool by 6.

A: Yuck, that sucks.

L: Used to it. Now it sucks not having to go.

A: Explain.

Linc contemplated Alexis' words. Fingers hovered over the keys prepared to type whatever popped into his head.

This is not a conversation to have over text.

L: Let's talk about it over dinner. What time will you be back?

With no immediate response, Linc placed the phone on his nightstand.

Where did you go, Pretty?

After several minutes, Linc climbed out of bed. He stuck his head out of the bathroom door, pretending to wait for the water to heat. No alert from his phone.

She must've started early.

Fresh out of the shower, Linc double-checked for missed texts, then took a quick glance at the clock. Impatient, he sat on the edge of his bed and wrestled with what to send. Before he could come with anything catchy, something that wouldn't sound stalker-ish, a text popped up.

Becks: Dude. Seth just called me. Your girl was just dropped off at the train station. He said she's pretty upset.

He scrolled up to Becks' number and pushed call. "What happened?"

"He didn't say," Becks replied without emotion.

"How long ago did he drop her off?"

"Within the last 10 to 15 minutes."

Frustration poured out of Linc. "Did he just leave her there?"

"Linc, it's fucking early as fuck here. I gave you all the info I got. He's a driver, not a counselor. Call your girl."

"Sorry, man. Thanks."

Linc scrolled to Alexis in his contacts and hit call.

Alexis answered on the second ring. "Hello."

"Hey. Is everything all right?" Linc asked slowly.

"If, by all right, you mean, they called and said there was no need for me to come back, then yes, everything is all right." Sadness filled her voice.

"Did they give you a reason?" he fished, as gently as he could. *Talk to me, Pretty.*

"None. Just that they had all they needed from the first day and that they could put me on an earlier train. I'm at the train station now."

"That sucks. I'm so sorry, Alexis."

"It's okay. I'm used to it. I guess my resume makes a better impression than I do."

"What time will you be back?"

"Ummm."

A rustling of paper made Linc smile.

"1:30 pm."

"I'll pick you up. We can get lunch."

"You don't have to, you know," Alexis replied, flatly.

She's shutting down again.

"I'll be there."

...

Linc was relieved to see JoAnne behind the counter. "Hi."

"Hello. What can I get you today?"

Linc appreciated her lack of flirting.

"Two large vanilla lattes, please."

She smiled knowingly. "Here, or to-go?"

"To go. Her train won't be in for another twenty minutes."

"So, what you want is two grande vanilla lattes, one extra hot." JoAnne said, with a wide smile. "Stick with me, I'll get you ordering like a pro in no time."

"I've got another pro-move I need your help on...Alexis'

75

favorite restaurant?"

She shrugged. "No clue."

Worth a try.

Placing a marker on the counter, JoAnne paused. "Hold on. We have discussed our common love for pasta."

"And, thank you very much for that. Italian is very helpful."

"Do you know how the trip went?" JoAnne asked, placing one cup inside another.

Linc forced a smile. "I'm waiting for all the details."

"Oh, that bad," she whispered, placing the cups on the counter.

"Why'd you put this one in another cup?"

"Double cup. It's the extra hot one. The sleeves don't work as well. Honestly, they just get it wrong. Double cup...that's the way to go."

"I like it...double cup."

JoAnne laughed. "You just like saying it."

"I won't forget that anytime soon." He could still hear her laughing as the door closed behind him.

Linc slowly rotated Alexis' latte in the car's drink holder.

Double Cup. That'd be an interesting name for a coffee place.

All thoughts evaporated with the knowledge of Alexis' arrival. Linc knew her scent would fill his car and that her smile would brighten his day. Alexis had an effect on him. And he liked it.

From where Linc stood, he could see all the exits off the train. His patience, wearing thin while he waited for the first sign of the girl who was changing him, finally eased as the conductors placed stepstools under each exit.

Alexis hadn't made it onto the platform before Linc reached for her bag. He smiled as he offered his hand for assistance. She hesitated for a split second, and then handed him her suitcase.

"Welcome back, Pretty."

"Thank you..."

Alexis cautiously stepped off the last step of the train. Once she was on solid ground, he squeezed her hand and led the way to the car.

"How was the train?"

"It was fine," Alexis responded, from half a step behind. "I slept mostly."

"I stopped at the coffee shop on the way."

Alexis slid into the seat and greeted the warm coffee like a long-lost friend. With her luggage stowed in the trunk, Linc climbed in next to her and pulled out of the station. "You look nice. Very nice."

And, smell so good.

Alexis lowered her head. "Thanks."

"So, you need to direct me to your place so we can drop off your bag. If you'd like to change, great. If not, great. After, let's go get pasta. Sound like a plan?"

"I needed this," Alexis said, as she sipped the coffee.

"Is it still warm?"

Alexis nodded.

"Double cup. Makes all the difference."

"That one." Alexis pointed at the brick apartment building on the right. "The apartment with the big light catcher in the window."

Light catcher?

"What's a light catcher?"

"The blue sphere hanging in the window that light dances through. It makes everything in my apartment colorful."

"Huh. I'll get your door, so hang on." He said, staring at the blue ball.

Seems odd for a Spartan not to have a green one.

Linc put the car in park, retrieved her luggage from the trunk, and popped her door open.

"I didn't have a chance to clean before I left, so it's a little disorganized," Alexis warned.

So, she's inviting me inside.

"Then we're even, because you've been to my house, and it wasn't exactly spotless and ready for visitors."

"Honestly, I was surprised at how clean it was." She laughed as she led Linc to the door.

I love that sound.

"Because I am a guy?"

Alexis laughed harder. "Yeah."

"I hate to ruin your impression of me, but I'm not going to lie to you."

Alexis tensed and stopped unlocking her door. All the light-heartedness had fled from her face.

"Okay, chill. I haven't killed anyone. I have a cleaning service that comes in twice a month. They started when Becks and I moved into the house. It's just easier."

"Someone cleans your house for you?"

You really don't know her facial expressions yet.

"And grocery shops and food prep."

"You're a COLLEGE STUDENT."

"Yeah, I'm also a college athlete. We train a lot. There are some things that need to be removed from our plates and taken care of by someone else."

"Really? Is that written somewhere? Or do they teach you all that at entitlement camp?"

Alexis pushed the door open and walked in.

Did she just say 'entitlement' camp? She did not just call you out. Why do you want to spend time with her?

"Come in. I'll hurry." Alexis disappeared through the only door in the room.

"Take your time, Alexis. We're not in a hurry."

Linc processed the 'entitlement' comment as he stepped into the apartment, but when the door closed softly behind him, her space became his sole focus.

He stood stunned when he realized her entire apartment, minus the bathroom, would fit in his living room. To add to the feeling of confined space, every surface of wall space was covered in maps. The center of the wall displayed a large world map, surrounded by maps of Turkey, Greece, Ireland, Portugal, Bali, Spain, and France. Pictures filled the small spaces between the maps.

This is intense.

Other than a couple of pieces of clothing spread across a futon, which brought haunting memories of sleepless filled nights in the dorm, the studio seemed neat and organized. For the size of the studio, Alexis had done a great job at laying out a floor plan with distinct sitting area, sleeping space, and desk area.

Linc worked to glean as much about Alexis from her apartment as possible. It was evident that orange was her color as it was used in a subtle way in each of the areas. The study area was covered floor to ceiling in quotes typed in big black block letters.

A large pile of books sitting on a make shift table caught Linc's attention. They were all destination themed. He sat in the chair and picked up a Chicago coffee table book. The few words he had read from Alexis' journal came racing back.

"...I can't fit in the fucking airplane seat..."

Dude, you can help her get in shape. You can start after graduation. Coach Dockett will help with a strength training program. This is going to be great.

"Sorry to keep you waiting."

Linc hadn't heard her come back in the room.

She wore a pink shirt that reached all the way to middle of her thighs and jeans that cuffed at the ankle. Linc noticed she gathered the front of her hair in a clip while the back fell loose down her back. Her makeup was gone. She looked so beautiful.

"Alexis, you look beautiful."

She glanced down at herself, and when her eyes met his, Linc saw a questioning look on her face.

"Thanks?"

"No, seriously. I don't like the makeup."

He thought he saw her blushing but she moved past him before he could tell.

"Ready?"

Linc remained seated. "I'd like to hear about your apartment."

Alexis wrinkled her nose. "This apartment?"

"Do you have another apartment?"

"Now? You did mention pasta."

"Touché."

Alexis held the door for Linc.

"So, Turkey?"

"Yeah, I've been a bit obsessed with Asia Minor since I first learned about it in high school."

Linc walked to the map and located the country in question. "I haven't heard it called that in a while. What about Asia Minor interests you?"

"The fact it went through so many transformations and each one contributed something significant to the world. It's a beautiful part of the world. I can't wait to visit the Hagia Sophia."

"Huh. I've never met a chi-lady that wanted to visit Turkey. You're so different. I'm glad we're friends." Linc passed through the doorway. "Let's eat."

CHAPTER 17

"Is this place okay, or would you rather try something else?" Linc whispered in Alexis' ear.

"I've never been here," she said looking around at everything.

"The pasta's really good."

Alexis nodded.

"Two, please," Linc said to the hostess, who smiled broadly back, and then led them to a booth.

"How's this?"

Alexis drew in a huge breath as her shoulders shot up to her ears and her back rounded.

Something's off. What's going on?

Slowly, Alexis reached for the back of the booth and lowered her body onto the bench seat. She moved her thigh slightly first to ensure the table impaled her in the most bearable spot. The hostess, watching Alexis attempting to maneuver, smiled.

Shit!

"Alexis, would you mind if we got a table? I think it will be better on my back."

When she looked up at him the light that Linc had gotten used to seeing bounce around in her eyes was absent. He turned his back to her to block anyone who might glance over from seeing her struggle out of the small space.

"We'd prefer a table," Linc snapped.

"Of course, right this way."

He claimed Alexis' hand and locked his fingers intertwined with hers, determined to make Alexis' comfort his sole priority.

This won't happen next time, Pretty. Dude, you have a lot to learn.

Linc scanned the restaurant as the pair was led to opposite side of the room. Tables had been equipped with a mix of chairs with arms and chairs without arms. He hadn't notice the aisles alternated in widths until they'd already scooted through one of the more narrow ones to reach the new table.

"Better?" The hostess asked, looking at Linc in a way that was much too familiar for someone on a date with another woman.

"Alexis." He gently tugged her closer to the table before letting go to pull out a chair without arms. "This is much better."

The hostess placed menus on the table and excused herself with one last smile and wink.

Really. Let's hope Alexis didn't see that.

"Do you get that everywhere you go?" Alexis asked, as she read over the menu.

Of course she caught it.

"Get what?"

She looked up and gave him a 'you know exactly what the fuck I'm referring to' look.

"I'm sure I don't get it any more than you do."

"Yeah, right."

"Anything look good? I always get the spaghetti. It's great."

Alexis smiled.

"What?"

"People getting the same thing when they go to a restaurant. My dad is like that. Every restaurant we used to go to he would always get the same thing."

He tried again. "Yeah, but the spaghetti is really good."

"Must be." Alexis giggled, and Linc relaxed.

"Welcome to Rotunno's." A waitress placed water glasses in front of each of them. "Do you know what you'd like or would you like a few more minutes?"

Linc looked up from the menu.

Alexis smiled.

Damn. There it is.

Linc couldn't help but to smile back at her. "Ready?"

"I'll try the spaghetti." She handed the menu to the waitress.

"Two spaghetti dinners, please. Do you want something to drink?"

"Water is fine for me. Thank you"

"Okay. Just the spaghetti, please."

The waitress nodded and departed promptly.

Clasping his hands together, "Should we talk about Chicago?"

Alexis' shoulders slumped and her head fell forward. "Not even a little bit."

"That bad?"

"That's what's so strange." Alexis sat up abruptly. "I didn't think it went badly at all. I walked into an interview with two execs, and within a matter of minutes, I felt very comfortable. They said they were impressed by my knowledge of Turkey and the Asian market as a whole. I even stated that I had plans to rule all of Asia Minor someday."

"And how did that go over?"

"They both laughed. We talked about my desire to live in Istanbul. Someone even came into the meeting at one point to tell the vice president we were over the allotted time. Warned him he was going to be late for his next meeting."

"Alexis, this sounds promising."

Alexis continued, using her hands accentuate her words. "I thought so, too. I got a quick tour of the offices, went to lunch with the current supervising manager of the Asia offices, and then I met with four other individuals to discuss where the company is heading over the next ten years. It was like a strategic brainstorm planning meeting all-in-one."

"I've never heard of that during the interview process."

Alexis took a sip of water. "It was informal. I'm guessing they used it to gauge my ability see the big picture and apply what I've learned in school to real world scenarios. Linc, it was fun to bounce ideas off the walls in the room and see where they would land. I sort of thought I held my own in there."

Could this all be because of her size? Is that possible?

"I'm sorry, Alexis."

"Yeah, me too. It just sucks." She said resignedly.

"You mentioned Plan B. What's Plan B?"

"How about you tell me about you for a change?" Alexis shot back.

Linc blinked in surprise. "What do you want to know?"

"I don't know. Swimming? Your plans after school?"

"Oh, so you want to start with the easy questions and work your way up to the difficult stuff like 'what's my favorite color?'"

She paused, "I mean, you have read my journal."

"Again, I haven't read your journal. I opened it to make sure it wasn't notes for a class. I determined it wasn't...I closed it immediately."

"Yeah, okay."

"Swimming. Huh."

Alexis smirked. "The pool is your favorite place on campus."

Why is that funny?

"Was. I swam the fly."

"Was? Fly?"

"Sorry. The butterfly. And, I say 'was' because my swimming career is over."

"The one with the arms?"

"Up until a couple of weeks ago, the butterfly was my life."

His eyes darted to his Pellegrino bottle and he began to pick at the label.

Dude, this is really hard to talk about. It's the end of swimming.

"Is this a conversation best saved for another time?"

"I'm sorry. I guess I'm still processing the end of my swimming career." Linc took a sip of his water. "I'd like to talk about it, later."

"Anytime."

The spaghetti arrived. Alexis placed a napkin on her lap, rested her chin on her palm, and asked, "So, Linc, what's your favorite color?"

"It's blue. Thanks for asking."

"Uh-huh. And, what are your plans after you graduate?"

He laughed, but hesitated to respond. "I'm not exactly sure yet."

Alexis waited expectantly with her fork poised over her plate.

Oh, she's totally going to make you keep going.

"I came here to swim. I love being on the pool deck. I love competing. I can't really imagine myself doing anything else."

She held up her hand for him to wait while she finished chewing and swallowed. "You came to Michigan State for an education. While you were here, you participated in swimming. College is for an education."

"In the beginning, I did come just to swim."

Alexis stifled her laugher. "I thought only athletes with the chance to go pro had that mindset. The players I've talked to are glad they're playing but their main goal is to walk out with that paper."

Is she right? Dude, you've been struggling with this for a while. She just threw it out all concisely and shit.

"What options are you considering?" She asked.

This is beginning to feel a little too much like an interview. And, you asked for this. Man up!!

"Many swimmers stick around the pool and find assistant coaching positions."

Alexis rolled her eyes. "Or..."

"Or, I could find a teaching position and teach swimming."

"And, remain around the pool," she said with a smile.

"High school coaching is a lot less competitive, but I'd still be on the pool deck."

"Interesting. What's involved with being an assistant coach?"

"For a entry-level assistant coach, recruiting. Lots and lots of recruiting. I'd drive around watching high school students swim and convince them to come to here to swim."

"Huh."

That doesn't sound good.

"What's, 'Huh?'"

"It just seems like you'd have more impact on a kid's life as a high school coach. You'd have the opportunity to develop them for a longer period of time before the craziness of college pressure gets placed on them." Alexis paused to take a bite. "You want to be by the pool. As a recruiter, it sounds like you'll spend most of your time away from the pool. Which are you leaning toward?"

Linc was speechless.

Alexis pointed at her plate. "This is really good."

Dude, over a plate of spaghetti, Alexis Kennedy Hewson has taken your two life choices and stripped away all the noise. Weeks of weighing the pros and the cons, and it all comes down to a couple questions over dinner.

CHAPTER 18

Don't call her. It's early. You just had dinner last night. Dude, don't pick up your phone. Do not call her!

Linc pushed his phone back into his locker, and then headed for the showers.

Where would you go anyway? You can't just call and not have a plan. She seems like a very 'have-a-plan' type of girl. Shit, dude, don't call. Captain Obvious. Let's give her one day of spring break to chill without you calling her.

As chlorine rinsed away from his body, Linc closed his eyes and pictured Alexis. His eyes popped open.

Note to self. Next time you imagine Alexis while in the shower, make sure it's in the privacy of your own home.

Back at his locker, Linc sent Alexis a text.

> Linc: Good morning. Would you like to go to the zoo with me today?
>
> Alexis: Morning. Seriously?
>
> L: Yes, I like zoos. Do you have a problem with the zoo?
>
> A: No. I just haven't been since I was a kid.
>
> L: What!!! You should go to the zoo with me. It'll be fun.
>
> A: Ummmmm...ok. I guess.
>
> L: Excellent. I'll pick you up in 30 mins with coffee.
>
> A: You should've opened with the coffee!! See ya.

JoAnne's warm smile greeted Linc when he entered the vacant coffee shop.

"Are you the only one who works here?" he joked, as he made his way to the counter.

"Feels like it this week. It's dead over the break, so it's easy money. What can I get you today?"

"Two vanilla lattes, please. Double cup."

JoAnne began grinning before all the words were out of his

mouth.

Quickly glancing over the numbers on his bills, Linc chose to keep one ten over another because it had a four eights.

That's a winner! Oh yeah. A date with Alexis and ordering the coffee in the 'preferred' manner, it's going to be a good day.

"Size first. Size, type of drink and, then, any extras. You'll get there...trust."

And, balls busted yet again by this one.

"I'm assuming by the vanilla lattes that one of these is for Alexis. So, shall I make them supers?"

Linc nodded. "Yes and yes, please."

JoAnne handed him back the change. Linc dropped it into the tip jar.

"You're quickly becoming my favorite customer, Linc."

"Oh yeah." Linc stood under the 'Pick up' sign. "Even though I don't order my drinks to your standards."

"See, that's your first mistake. They're not really my standards, Swimmer Boy. It's just how it is."

He clutched his chest. "Swimmer boy...this, after I tipped you."

"It'll cost you a lot more for me to not make fun of you. What's the plan for today? Since she won't be coming in to keep me company, thank you very much."

"We're going to the zoo."

"Huh."

Now, what?

"Huh, what?"

"Huh, nothing."

"Okay." He watched her work the coffee machine.

"For real, though, Linc. The zoo?"

"What?"

"You know Alexis is big, right?"

He shook his head in an effort to wrap his mind around her comment. "What does that even mean?"

"People suck!" she replied, forcefully.

"Okay, I'm not getting this at all."

"First, Alexis has spent all of her time staying close to home, surrounded by people that accept her or situations she's equipped to handle."

"Accept her for what?"

JoAnne raised her hand in Linc's face to stop him. "WAIT!"

He leaned against the counter and waited.

"People who accept her and don't judge her on her size. You know, unlike your asshole friends. Or don't you recall the doing charity work comment? Second, all the walking might be hard for her. You're Mr. Swimmer Boy and she's, well, not. How's she going to keep up at the zoo?"

"Did she talk to you about us going to the zoo–"

Rolling her eyes dramatically, JoAnne continued, "Finally, what if people make fun of her?"

Straightening up, Linc picked up the coffees JoAnne had placed on the counter in front of him.

"Let's see if I understand your concerns. Alexis getting made fun of by mean people, and me not being aware that her level of fitness is lower than mine. Does that sum it up?"

"You're completely oversimplifying." She shot him an evil glare and crossed her arms.

Linc laughed. "I'm only trying to balance the scale with your over dramatic worries of a simple trip to the zoo."

Creased brow, tensed shoulders, and sad eyes, JoAnne didn't believe things would be better than she thought, or that Alexis would have an amazing day with him.

He began his defense. "A. I'll be with her the entire time. No one is going to say anything out of line."

His hand flew up to stop JoAnne from saying anything. "B. I'm not an oblivious ass. I understand we're not in the same shape. Not many people are in the shape I'm in."

"Forget it." The sadness in her words told him Alexis meant a lot to her.

"Okay. Okay. C. And most importantly, I want to spend the day with your friend. I chose the zoo because I happen to love zoos. We could sit at that table over in Alexis' comfort zone for the day, and I'd still be geeked."

JoAnne's face slowly relaxed, and a huge smile replaced her pursed lips.

"Now what?"

Chicks are so weird. Shit, girls are so weird.

"You're starting to like Alexis. I mean, K I S S I N G kind of like her."

What are we, twelve? Seriously, I'm not being called out on this.

"JoAnne, I've listened, I've heard, and now I'm taking your friend to the zoo. You'll see. It'll be great."

This is crazy! Alexis can't have to deal with this shit every day. How much walking? People being mean. Shit, the hostess. That was shitty. Damn, maybe the zoo wasn't a great idea.

Halfway out the door, he almost dropped the coffees at JoAnne's famous last words.

"I'll kick your ass if she gets hurt. They won't find you if you hurt her."

The zoo. All I want to do is take a girl to the zoo.

CHAPTER 19

"We don't have to go to the zoo." The words blurted out as Alexis opened her door. Linc, confident of only one thing, held up the latte.

"Okay. Thanks?"

"I love zoos. I thought it'd be a fun day. Something fun to do together."

Alexis started, "Ummmm–"

"But, if you're uncomfortable with the idea...we can do something else," Linc interrupted.

She's smiling behind her cup. Why is she smiling? What does that mean? Shit...JoAnne was right.

She took another sip, then started again. "Well–"

"What would you rather do? Name it."

"Finish a sentence."

"Huh." That caught him off-guard.

"You keep cutting me off. I haven't finished a sentence yet. Although, this is the first time I've witnessed you off balance." Alexis moved to the side, making room for Linc to enter her apartment.

She sat on her futon, which was now in couch position, and drank her coffee. As he returned to the same chair as before, Alexis' scent surrounded him like a blanket.

Damn. She smells so good. What is it with her? Pull it together, Dude. This is not your first rodeo.

"Your hair looks nice today. I mean, you look really nice today."

"Thank you," she replied softly. Her smile was gone, and her shoulders lifted closer to her ears. She no longer looked at Linc, but instead, watched the floor.

"Alexis. About the zoo. Seriously. We don't have to go to the zoo. It isn't that big of a deal."

Playing with the lid on her coffee, she still hadn't looked at him since he had complimented her.

"I can't remember the last time I went to the zoo. I was thinking about it while I was getting ready, and I really couldn't remember." She sipped her coffee and searched his eyes. "May I ask why you're offering me an out?"

"Let me be very clear, I was offering you an out for the zoo, not for the day. I very much want to spend the day with you."

She sat silently.

"When I stopped to get coffee, JoAnne mentioned the zoo might be a bad idea."

"That's odd. I can almost guarantee she and I've never had a conversation about zoos. Did she give you any reason?"

Shit. Okay, asshole, what do you say now? This is one of those defining moments. Tread carefully.

"She's very protective of you, Alexis. JoAnne wanted to ensure you're treated well. I think her concern is the zoo might not be a place you'd choose to spend time."

Alexis laughed. "It's not."

"We don't have to go," he said quietly.

"I'd like to."

"Yeah?"

"Yep, I'm planning on being Kennedy today," she replied with a bright smile.

Sweet Jesus, Alexis. Really love that smile!

Linc smiled. "Kennedy, huh? I've created something here?"

Alexis stood and looked down at him confidently. "I think you may have. We shall see."

"I'm as eager to get to know Kennedy as I am Alexis."

Linc followed Alexis to the door. Outside, he slid his sunglasses into place and grabbed her hand. She hesitated at first, but Linc laced his fingers with hers and led her to the car.

Oh, Pretty, you are going to have to get used to this.

Linc turned the radio on as they turned out of the parking lot. *You're Beautiful* played softly in the background. Within minutes, they sped down the ramp to the expressway.

Alexis looked around. "Is this how you get to Potter Park?"

"Potter Park isn't a real zoo," Linc asserted. "We're going to the Toledo Zoo."

"Toledo! The one in Ohio?"

"Yes, Ma'am."

"We are going to Ohio?" she rephrased.

"Yep. Problem?" Linc gauged her response, ready to return home if she protested too strongly.

"Not a problem. I guess." She said, with a loud exhale. "I'm just surprised."

"The Toledo Zoo rocks. You haven't been to a zoo in like, forever, so I thought a bigger zoo was in order. Okay?"

Linc heard the wheels churning in her head.

"Okay."

Linc took her hand and placed it on his thigh, then kept a firm hold. "Plus, it gives us lots of time in the car together. Road trips are a great way to get to know someone."

"Because you're trapped," Alexis mumbled, staring out the window.

"Or because there are no interruptions."

She giggled. "Oh, okay. That too."

"So, Kennedy. Would you like to start, or would you like me to ask the first question? Answer carefully. My question is a doozy."

Alexis removed her hand from his thigh. She shifted so her back was against the door.

"This was your plan the entire time," she accused.

"What?"

This should be good.

"To get me in a place where I couldn't leave, and ask me tough questions."

"Busted. You figured me out. My goal all along has been to get to know you, and my plan to do so is to ask you questions."

Alexis rolled her eyes and straightened in her seat. "Smartass."

"It'll be a long boring drive if we just sit here and listen to the radio."

"Are you sure?" she grumpily tossed out.

"Completely. And, I'm considering that your first question. My turn."

"Ummmm … no. That wasn't my question. It wasn't even a question."

"Splitting hairs."

"No. Correcting you."

"If that wasn't your question, what is your question then?" Linc goaded.

"What would you like to be remembered for by your college friends?"

"That's your question? What do I want to be remembered for? Okay. Not really a question I was expecting."

Alexis' laughter filled the car as they sped down I-96.

This is going to be a great day.

CHAPTER 20

"My treat."

"Are you sure? You bought dinner last night." She held out her cash.

"Put your money away! Today is completely on me."

Alexis shook her head and pocketed her money.

"What's your favorite exhibit at this zoo?" she asked, as she opened the zoo map.

"Hippos and polar bears." He answered without hesitation. "I love walking around the zoo. It's a happy place. My parents used to bring us to the zoo when we were very young."

Alexis snorted. "I wonder if the animals think it's a happy place."

"Well, zoos are used for conservation, so the animals are extremely well-cared for."

"Still."

"There are some shitty zoos, but for the most part, zookeepers work hard to ensure the animals are happy."

"You seem to be interested in zoos. Why didn't you go into animal studies instead of education?" Alexis said, as he handed her a ticket.

"My mother felt education was the furthest below the expected standard I could sink, and they'd still pay for it. There's no possible way working with animals would've been acceptable." Sadness filled his words.

"What was the expected area of study?"

Staring into the lion exhibit, Linc contemplated Alexis' question for a minute. "Political Science."

"Really?"

Linc nodded. "Herbert Lincoln James."

"Presidential candidate material. I get it. Yikes, there's some pressure."

"Just a little."

Alexis connected the dots. "Is that why you started swimming? Looks good on a campaign poster?"

"Just the opposite," Linc said. "I needed an escape from my mother and her directing everything I did. This one day, I was supposed to start music lessons at school. The high school swim coach was at the middle school to start a junior swim team. I mentioned I didn't have a bathing suit, so he let me wear a team suit. I never made it to the music class, and I never learned to play an instrument. I was too young for the team, but the coach saw something in me. My dad and sister were excited for me. Grace, my sister, came to almost all of my meets over the years."

"What about your mother?"

He shook his head. "She wasn't happy. She didn't want me to stay in swimming because it wasn't a straight line to the White House. To make it worse, I chose to come to State to swim which is definitely not any kind of line to the White House."

"Do you want to go into politics?"

"No. It was never something I saw myself doing. Ironically, I think my sister would make a kickass president."

"Why?"

"Grace has always had her shit together. She has a vast knowledge of everything important, and she cares about people."

"And you don't?"

Linc led her to the next exhibit. "I have a vast knowledge of useless information."

"I take it you and your sister are close."

"Yeah, we are. It's always been she and I against my mother's plans for us."

"Do you see your sister often?"

"Grace is in Italy at the moment, working on a plan to bring energy to third world countries."

"Wow."

Alexis turned away from the giraffes to look at Linc. He was already looking at her.

"Yep, she is impressive."

Linc grabbed her hand and pulled her toward his favorite part of the zoo. The hippos.

Alexis tensed and lost a step. He squeezed her hand harder.

"Does it bother you when I hold your hand?"

Alexis stopped in her tracks. She kept her eyes forward, but didn't pull away. "Ummmmm...not really."

Stepping into her personal space, Linc continued to press. "Let me rephrase, would you prefer me not to hold your hand?"

She looked at him.

What does that look mean?

Alexis glanced around as if she had misplaced something. Linc followed, trying to see what she was looking for.

"No," she said, in almost a whisper.

"What's wrong?"

"I guess I'm just wondering why you want to."

"What? Hold your hand?"

Alexis nodded.

How do you answer that question? You want to be close. You want all the other guys to know she's with you. Be honest. Dude, you need to pump your brakes. Don't say any of that.

Linc answered honestly. "It just feels right. Would you rather I didn't?"

"It's fine. I just don't want people to talk about you," she said.

"What? I don't give a shit about anyone in here but you."

"Come on. Let's go this way."

Walking to the monkey house hand in hand, they didn't talk. Alexis seemed lost in thought.

Just tell her you want to be close to her. Dumbass.

A crowd had gathered in the monkey house. Alexis watched a little snow monkey, and it watched her right back. Linc moved off to the side, slipped his phone from his pocket, and captured a smiling Alexis in several shots. Her head tilted back, and he snapped another photo of her mid-laugh.

Linc moved behind Alexis to whisper in her ear. "Hey, let's take a picture."

She spun, ending up in Linc's arms. Her eyes grew round and her mouth was agape. She looked around before speaking. "Ummmmm...okay."

He positioned the camera so they were both centered in the camera lens. Linc kept clicking pictures. With the volume off, Alexis had no idea he had begun, and she finally, relaxed into his chest.

"Tell me when."

"Now," Linc said, as he kissed her on the cheek.

Alexis giggled and leaned closer into him. He laughed, and held her tighter.

"What the hell is he doing with her?" someone said to the left of Linc. "Did you know there's a cow at the zoo?"

Linc tensed, and he pulled her closer. He wasn't going to let her go in an attempt to shield her from any hurt.

Are you shitting me? That did not just happen.

A smiling Alexis looked up. "Ready?"

CHAPTER 21

Dude, you have to calm down. How is she not losing it? Don't be an asshole! Refocus.

Linc smiled. "This is my favorite exhibit of all of them. If I timed it right, we are just in time for the scrubbing."

"The what?"

They slowly walk around a bend in the path. He pointed into the enclosure. "Wait for it."

Excellent! Just in time.

"So, I think this is really cool."

Linc pulled Alexis back into his arms, feeling the need to shield her from other petty zoo visitors.

"...look," Alexis pointed and laughed.

For the first time, Linc's happy place wasn't the pool, it was standing in front of the hippo exhibit, holding Alexis in his arms, and feeling the vibration of her laugh on his chest.

The zookeeper had been scrubbing the scum off the glass of the aquarium when a hippo came up and opened its gaping jaw. The keeper brushed the hippo's big tongue. Two other hippos made their way over and opened their mouths, begging for some brush time as well. Seeing this, Alexis laughed harder.

Linc leaned in to whisper into Alexis' ear. His lips got within a centimeter of her neck allowing her scent to hijack his thoughts. "You smell so good."

"Thanks. It's just lotion."

"I like it," Linc said, releasing her.

"Looks like a hippo escaped the enclosure," a stranger mocked. Linc turned to identify who made the shitty comment.

Oh, hell no! Little Pussies!

Three teenage boys stood behind them laughing. Alexis ignored the comment, but Linc struggled with letting them go.

"Be right back," he whispered in her ear.

"Please don't," Alexis begged, holding Linc back. From inside his arms, she shielded the petty zoo visitors from him.

"Alexis."

She hadn't taken her eyes off the hippos. Her body was in the same relaxed state it had been in before the asshole made the comment.

Alexis suggested, "Let's just go and see what's next."

Linc glanced to see if they were still there, but the little asshats had moved on.

What the hell? This is ridiculous. How is she okay? This shit isn't right.

"Let's get something to drink. Hotdog?" he tried.

Alexis looked at Linc with a forced smile. He took her hand, and they walked to the concession stand.

"Do they have otters?" Alexis asked, hopefully.

He smiled down at her. "Yep, are you a fan?"

"Yeah, they crack me up when they play."

How is she not freaking out?

"Nice." Linc said, surprised the word slipped out.

"What?"

Linc pointed to the sign to the left of Alexis. "They have corndogs."

"Awww...I love corndogs."

Linc laughed.

Alexis watched him closely. "Hey, you were commenting on something else. Tell me."

"I can't think of anything but corndogs. I smell them now."

"I'll let this one go but only because I can't remember what I said to question your remark, also because I can't recall due to the smell of those corndogs."

"After you, Ms. Alexis."

"You might have to start calling me Kennedy." The humor in Alexis' voice vanished when she saw Linc's serious expression.

They squeezed in at the back of the line. Linc pulled Alexis back into his chest and wrapped his arms around her. "No wonder this place feels like it's half empty. Everyone's in here trying to eat."

Dude, you have got to hold it together. How's she so calm when asshats are talking about her to her face.

The line moved up, they stepped together. "This may not be so bad." Alexis remained calm while Linc felt his anxiety increasing.

He scanned the crowd.

Don't even look at her? Look away, asshole.

Several minutes later, with corndog combos and an extra bag filled with ketchup and mustard, Linc led Alexis to a small cluster of tables out back.

"Yes, overflow seating options."

Alexis followed him to a table. She smiled the same forced smile as before.

Did someone say something? Dude, you didn't even hear it if they did. Shit!

"You okay?" He asked, as she poured herself into the picnic table seating.

"Great. Still not interested in trying mustard on my corndog."

"You will love it. Guaranteed."

Waves of visitors strolled by while Linc and Alexis ate in silence and watched the merriment in front of them. A screaming kid, adamant that a trip to the restroom was unnecessary, made them laugh while the frustrated father shrugged his shoulders in defeat.

Two colorful peacocks meandered by the table, and Linc broke the silence. "So, can I ask a question?"

"I kind of thought that's what we've both been doing," Alexis said as he snapped pictures of the birds on his phone.

"You know what I mean."

She clarified. "You mean, can you ask me a difficult question? One that might upset me?"

"Well, now that you put it that way, forget it." Linc looked at Alexis, who was doing her best to avoid eye contact.

"Oh come on, that's just how it always starts doesn't it?"

How what starts? This went down a dark road quickly.

"I want to get to know you, that's all."

Alexis wadded up the last of her wrappers.

"Did I mention I would also buy you coffee later?"

She dropped the trash in her hand on the table and leaned in toward Linc. "Ask away."

Without hesitation, the words spilled out of his mouth. "Does it bother you when I compliment you?"

"Wow. That's a direction I wasn't expecting." Alexis sat up straight. Her eyes searched for anything to stare at besides the man sitting across from her.

"What were you expecting?"

Linc watched Alexis's demeanor change before is his eyes. Her shoulders slumped, and she cast her gaze downward. "For you to ask me about people yelling things about my weight."

"Why? The problem is clearly with the individual with the small and simple personality. If you ever want to discuss how it makes you feel, I'm ready to listen, but that's on you to bring it up."

Linc gathered all the trash off the table. He felt her watching him as he walked to the trashcan. The half-smile she used to cover her thoughts was firmly back in place. "It would have been easier than the question you asked."

Linc sat next to her and shrugged. "Life's not about easy."

"Tou-fucking-ché," Alexis quipped.

Oh, yeah. Stealing that.

"Would you tell me why my compliments bother you?"

"It's not so much that they bother me. I'm just not accustomed to being complimented by men. Like, not even regular men," she answered softly.

Regular men. Oh, this is going to be interesting.

"Regular men." Linc leaned in closer. "What does that make me?"

"Whatever. Fishing much?"

Fishing. Dude, don't let her know you have zero idea what she's talking about. But, what the hell?

"Fishing?"

"Anyway, I'm not used to it."

Linc was quiet while he waited for a large group of people to pass.

"Have you dated? Been in relationships?" he inquired.

"I wouldn't call it dating, and I probably wouldn't classify them as relationships."

He stared at Alexis for a moment before continuing. "You do know your responses open the door to more questions.

"Don't most people's?"

"Not that I've experienced. I'm usually going over my swimming strokes by now." It was Linc's turn to avoid eye contact.

"I'm sorry?"

"When a situation becomes unbearable, I transport myself into the pool and breakdown each phase of the fly in my head. Where my hands are in the water relative to my body. I don't do that when I'm talking to you."

Alexis smiled. "Huh. I replay different games I've watched. Plays. Players tell."

"Your tune-out sounds more interesting than mine." His admission gave her a good laugh.

That laugh. Okay, but damn. You're not that funny. What's she laughing at? She's totally laughing at you.

Alexis was still laughing when she asked, "Are we done talking about this? You talked up this zoo experience pretty high."

"Tou-fucking-ché." Linc grabbed both water bottles.

"Don't start using my word."

It took everything for him to keep a straight face. "I might have to."

She giggled all the way to the next exhibit.

CHAPTER 22

Linc had slowed their pace considerably by the time they passed through the zoo exit. Sweat had gathered on Alexis' brow, and he watched a droplet slide down her cheek.

Maybe this was a bad idea.

Alexis smiled at Linc as he held the car door open for her. She retrieved her small purse stowed in the console, removed a tissue, then wiped her forehead. "Well, that was fun."

Linc started the car. "Really?"

"Yeah, I enjoyed it. Thank you."

He smiled at her. "Excellent. Thanks for agreeing to come with me."

"I'm a tad surprised you didn't have major plans for spring break."

"Yeah, well. I'm just a regular guy," he shot back. "Are you ever going to explain that comment?"

The laughter gave him his answer but she didn't leave him hanging. "Chances are slim."

"Fine."

"What are you doing tomorrow?" Alexis asked, as she scrolled through her phone.

YES! YES! YES!! Be cool. Be cool.

"Something with you. You pick."

"Oooo...I'm on it." She pushed buttons on her phone, and he watched her excitement grow.

After a couple minutes, she set her phone on her leg. American Pie filled the car, and Alexis started singing. She paused in the middle. "I love this song."

Linc smiled and turned the volume up.

As the song ended, Alexis casually said, "It reminds me of my dad."

Not wanting to miss a word, Linc turned the volume down to

quietly fill in the background.

"We used to drive to Florida to visit his family on holiday vacations. That's one of the songs he would sing." The bouncy fun in Alexis' voice had shifted to sad and introspective.

"Just you and your dad?" Linc wanted to reach for Alexis' hand.

"Nope, my mom and sister, too."

"You haven't talked about your family much. That's not a good subject for you?"

"There's not really much to talk about. I have a mother that doesn't support the decisions I'm making for my life, and a sister that has no use for a fat sibling."

Ouch! Okay, there's more to that.

"And your dad?"

"My dad." Alexis sighed. "My dad is the best father a girl like me could ask for. He loves me unconditionally and has always been my only cheerleader."

"I found out at sixteen that he wasn't really my father. Biologically, that is. Apparently, I'm the result of a one-night stand my mother felt she needed to have. Not the best news when you idolize your dad."

"Do you know your biological father?"

"I never asked. Kind of felt like, if that information wasn't shared with me, then maybe I could pretend it was false."

Linc couldn't imagine how she felt. "That has to be tough."

"It sucks," Alexis replied. "The really shitty part is, my sister told me in the middle of an argument."

"Which means she knew before you. Ouch!"

"Yeah, ouch. It was an argument about not wanting me in her wedding. She said I was too fat. I'd ruin the aesthetics." Alexis got quiet and stared at the dashboard in front of her.

"Did you tell her she wasn't going to be in your wedding?"

Screw them!

"She started laughing. She said no one would ever marry me. I was too fat. Then, she blurted out, 'your real dad didn't even want you.' Course, that wasn't far enough, she ended it with, 'He probably knew you were going to turn into a huge piece of nothing.'"

"Respectfully, your sister sounds like a royal bitch."

"She and I don't really have a relationship now. When she married, she moved to Florida with her husband. We haven't spoken in over three years."

"She's wrong, you know."

Alexis' head turned from the window to Linc, waiting for him to finish.

"You wouldn't have ruined anything at her wedding. And there will be a wedding in your future."

"Nah. I don't think so."

Linc was puzzled. "Why do you say that?"

"I don't want marriage. I've watched so many people in my extended family get married only to end in divorce. Shit, I'm a product of my mom not being faithful in her marriage. I have too much sense to fall into that trap."

"What about kids?"

"Ummmmm...NO!"

"I thought every woman wanted to grow up, get married, and have lots of kids."

"HA! You, my friend, thought wrong."

"What's the alternative?" he asked, blown away.

The back of her hand slapped the other to punctuate her point. "Get a great education. Find a job. Work hard. Move up the career ladder."

"Sounds lonely."

"Perhaps, to some." Alexis smiled. "But it sounds exciting to me."

"What if you meet the perfect guy? And he wants marriage and a family?"

"Then, he isn't the perfect guy for me...is he?"

"You are unique."

Alexis turned the table. "What about you? Are you one of those guys that want to get married and have lots of kids?"

"Unfortunately. Not anytime soon, of course, but I do want to have a home, wife, and kids someday."

Alexis returned to her phone. The radio no longer lingered in the background. It filled the gulf that formed between them.

Awkward. Say something. Dude, change the subject.

"Okay, about tomorrow–"

"Canceling on me already?" he asked.

She giggled. "Ummmm...no."

Linc was relieved she still wanted to see him and eager to hear her plan. "Good. What about tomorrow?"

Still focused on her phone, Alexis suggested, "We could go watch State practice."

"Practice. Season's over."

"Football, Silly."

"Football?" Linc echoed. "Football practice is closed until the Green and White game."

"Ish. Practice is closed to the public until the Green and White game." Alexis continued to mess with her phone with a smirk on her face.

"Pretty, if you have a way to get us into MSU's closed football practice–"

Alexis held up her finger and answered her phone. "Straight bets, nothing less than fifty, site goes up twenty-four hours before kickoff and down four hours later."

So, she is running numbers. How has this never come up?

She continued her phone call. "No. Okay. Okay. Thanks."

Alexis ended her call and returned the phone to her knee. Linc straightened in his seat, waiting for Alexis to explain.

"Should we meet at the stadium at 4pm? They have pictures tomorrow so they're running it late," Alexis stated confidently.

"You realize it's hard to stare at you and not crash, right?" Linc looked at Alexis, and then quickly returned his eyes to the road.

"What?"

Is she kidding?

He did a double take. "You're a bookie."

Alexis shrugged. "I dabble."

"In what, running a betting site and taking bets in an organized manner?"

Alexis smiled. "That's exactly what I dabble in."

Sensing she wasn't ready to open up about her enterprise, Linc reluctantly changed the subject. "By the way, the team picture gets taken on the day of the Green and White."

"Not the team picture, individual shots for the program and print promo material."

"I'll pick you up at 3 pm so we can get something to drink before."

"Not sure I'll be home by 3 pm, hence me suggesting we meet at the stadium," Alexis clarified, looking out the window.

"So, date with someone else during the day or something?" Linc fought to keep his eyes on the road.

"I'm volunteering at the shelter."

"Shelter?"

She explained, "The animal shelter, or pound, as most people refer to it."

Jesus, this chick is a saint. Lady! This lady is a saint. And, she smells good.

"What do you do?"

"Mostly, I just sit and pet the dogs."

"Aren't you a good person," Linc joked.

"Just doing my part. Plus, I've always wanted a dog. I can't have one in my apartment. Spending time at the shelter helps."

The trip back to Alexis' apartment building didn't take long enough for Linc. He wasn't done talking to her. He didn't know when he would be.

Ask her to dinner. Do it!

"Thanks for the trip to the zoo. I had a great time." She opened the door before he could mention dinner.

"Wait." Linc reached into the backseat for the stuffed hippo. "Don't forget this guy."

"How could I forget this cutie? Thank you for getting it for me. It'll remind me of the zoo."

It's supposed to remind you of me.

Linc held his hands to his chest. "And me."

"You, Sir, are hard not to think about." With that, she exited the car and headed for her front door.

Linc caught up with her and followed the remaining few feet. He waited as she opened the door. "That's great to hear."

Alexis giggled and stepped inside.

That's great to hear?!? What kind of dumbass comeback was that. Say something smooth...dinner.

"Thanks again...I'll see you tomorrow at the stadium."

"It's a date," he said firmly.

"A date. Later," she said, as she closed the door.

That was definitely not smooth. You get negative smooth points.

CHAPTER 23

Don't call her! Come on, Dude. Stay strong. You know you're going to see her this afternoon.

Water dripped on the locker room floor as Linc opened his locker and picked up his phone hoping for a message from Alexis.

MESSAGES!! Yes.

> Harrison: Man, you are missing out. So much fun! Check out my spring break honey.

Linc rolled his eyes and deleted the message. Reading Alexis' name, his head began to bob with enthusiasm before opening the message.

> Alexis: Good morning. Thank you again for a great day yesterday.

Yes. She had fun. Dude, play it cool. Simply reply. Just say hello.

He replied back, forgetting the conversation he had had with himself to not call.

> Link: Morning. I am just getting out of the pool. How about I bring you some coffee and tag along to the shelter?

Oh yeah, that's playing it cool. Still deducting smooth points, dipshit. Take a shower. You're totally pushing too hard.

Linc dropped his head forward and tossed his phone back in his locker. Alexis hijacked his thoughts again as cold water cascaded down his body.

What is it about her? You are off your game completely. Dude, when she was looking at that little monkey, she was so focused. Her smile. Shit, when she laughed.

"Okay, Dude. Shower time is definitely over. Again, think about Alexis at home."

Back at his locker, Linc avoided checking his phone until he was dressed and out of the building.

So much for a relaxing swim.

Linc waved to one of the maintenance guys as he tossed his towel in a bin. His thoughts still cloudy with Alexis, he sprinted out the exit and jogged the mile and a half home.

Linc flopped on his bed and finally granted himself permission to check for messages.

No message.

Probably shouldn't have been so pushy with the 'I'll come with you' and simply sent a 'good morning' text instead. Now what?

> A: Coffee sounds amazing. I'm just out of the shower so can you give me another 30?

Ah, man. You've got it bad. She was in the damn shower.

> L: See ya in 30 with coffee.

> A: I'm going to owe you a lot of coffee. Wear something old, the dogs will be all over you.

> L: It's worth every penny to see how happy a cup of coffee can make you.

> A: I do enjoy coffee

Linc broke several rules of the road to arrive at the coffee shop in record time. The place was empty. Eager to tell JoAnne about the successful trip to the zoo, he threw his car in park and hopped out almost before the tires had stopped turning.

As he walked in, he shouted, "I was right about the zoo!"

"What were you right about? Zoos are kind of lame, in my opinion." Shelley stood up and greeted him with an 'I want to eat you' smile.

"Oh, hey. Where's JoAnne?" Linc asked loudly, hoping she would pop out from the back.

"She had an appointment this morning, but I'm positive I can assist you with whatever you need."

Linc thought he should admire this chick's dedication to reaching her goal, but he didn't. "Thanks. I'll take a super big vanilla latte for Alexis and a large regular coffee with cream. Oh, double cup them, too."

He handed her a ten.

"I'm in town for the rest of break. Want to go to dinner tomorrow night?" she asked in her syrupy-sweet tone as she gave him back his change.

"I'm seeing Alexis," he reminded her.

"Muffin Girl?" Shelley scoffed. "Why?"

"Please don't refer to Alexis as Muffin Girl."

"Why are you settling for someone that looks like that when you could–"

"I could what?" Linc interrupted.

"You're hot! You could go out with anyone on campus. Fuck, I just asked you out, and I never do that." She reached for a paper cup to prepare the order.

He tried to explain so it was clear. "I'm going out with someone I'm interested in."

"She's fat. I mean super fat. You can't possibly be attracted to her." She placed a lid on each coffee. "What's the joke?"

"The joke is, I'm into her and not interested in seeing anyone else."

Shelley looked disgusted as she set the cups in front of Linc.

"Thanks for the coffee. When did you say JoAnne would be back?"

"Noon," she barked.

"Great, thanks."

Linc headed for the door.

"Hey, if you're doing this for some charity thing, I get it. We can hook up later if you want."

He turned around and returned to the counter. "I'm not sure what you mean by a 'charity thing,' but I'm going to be very clear here. I'm totally and completely interested in Alexis. I'm not looking to hook up with you now or later. Got it?"

Stunned, Shelley nodded.

Good." He walked out the door.

What the hell? We can hook up later? Are you kidding me? What a piece of work. Way to support your fellow woman too.

...

With his hands full, Linc lightly kicked Alexis' door.

"One sec!"

When the door opened, Linc peeked through a large green plant in time to see Alexis' eyes get big.

"Ummmm...okay," she pushed out.

"For you. And me too."

She laughed.

YES! So worth it.

"Come in." Alexis stepped out of the way. She clutched the coffee like it was a bouquet on the morning of the bride's wedding. "Yum."

"Coffee is really your thing, huh?"

"Coffee is my drinkable happy place." Alexis closed the door. "Have a seat."

"You smell so good."

"Thanks. It's still just lotion."

"I like it."

She looked away, but not before he caught her smiling.

"Here." Linc handed her the big green plant he had carried in with everything else. "This is clearly for you."

"Thank you so much," she whispered. "I don't really know what to say."

"I didn't know your favorite, but I thought this one was nice."

"I've never gotten a plant or flowers before," she whispered, as she stared at the plant.

"That's impossible. Your past boyfriends didn't buy you flowers?"

Alexis's shrugged, still looking at the plant. "As I said, I wouldn't really call them boyfriends."

"I brought McDonald's too. I'm starving."

Alexis shook her head. "No thanks. I never eat breakfast. Just coffee."

No past boyfriends. Interesting, or red flag?

"Breakfast is the most important meal of the day. Break – Fast...you are literally breaking your fast from the night before." Linc unwrapped a biscuit and took a big bite. "Bodies need calories to rev up and start the day. Not just coffee."

Alexis moved around the apartment with the plant still in her hands. Finally, she located the perfect spot on a little table next to her couch.

"Do you know you brought me a death plant?" she asked.

Linc froze.

She worked to suppress her smile.

"Huh?"

Alexis held the straightest face she could and explained. "It's a

Peace Lily. They're for funerals, or what you send when someone dies."

He stared at the plant. "Are you kidding me?"

"Nope. The first time I get a plant from a guy...death flowers." She slapped her hand over her mouth to keep the giggles from seeping out.

"I don't think it's funny," Linc pouted.

Without hesitation, Alexis countered, "Oh, it's a little funny."

"I was trying to do something different. Most guys would just bring you flowers, and they would die in a couple of days. I wanted to give you something that would live–"

Alexis put her hands up and got serious. "First, you are the first guy to ever give me a plant or flowers. Ever! Second, I'm laughing because I love Peace Lilies and think it's a shame they're known as death flowers. Third, thank you for getting me a plant. I will try really hard not to kill it."

He looked at the plant. "Then it really would be a death plant."

Alexis cracked up as she sat on her futon couch. Linc held up a bacon, egg, and cheese biscuit for her, but she lifted her coffee and continued to laugh.

"Eat it. Your body will love me for it," he insisted.

Alexis looked at Linc. She accepted the wrapped biscuit and slowly opened it.

"So, what will we be doing at the shelter?"

CHAPTER 24

Linc winked at Alexis as he approached the table with their beverages.

"What's that?" Alexis inquired, as Linc sat a red iced drink on the table.

"Rachel suggested I try it. It's a berries quencher or something."

Alexis threaded her fingers through the handle of the mug filled with her favorite vanilla latte. "You have fun with that."

"Speaking of fun, I've had a great time this week! I'm still surprised you got us into, not one, but two closed football practices."

"I'm shocked you got me to go golfing."

Linc laughed. "Again, it's called miniature golf, and you know it. You're not getting credit for real golf."

Alexis giggled and asked, "Were the football practices your favorite of the week?"

"Nah, meeting Gage, the world's greatest dog trapped at the pound was the best. I didn't believe you when you said it would be hard to leave because the first time it wasn't."

"Then, Gage," they said in unison.

Linc whispered, "He needs a good home. Soon."

Alexis nodded, as she stared at her coffee.

"I'd been dreading this week since figuring out I wasn't going to Keys. So, thank you," he said.

"Ummmm...you're welcome. I think. Dreading?"

"Yeah, missing the last trip with my friends."

"Ah." Alexis nodded. "Those wonderful friends of yours."

"The funny thing is, I'd never trade this spring break for a trip to the Keys."

"Why's that?"

"You," Linc answered without thought.

Linc stretched his hand across the table. Alexis placed her hand in his and he closed his fingers around hers. She smiled at him.

"I've had a great week. Thank you for being there during the Chicago thing. That was kind of you." Sadness rang in Alexis' voice.

The entire week had flown by without Alexis opening up about Chicago. To Linc, it felt like ages ago. The subject stopped coming up after the zoo, and the time they had shared had felt magical. He'd never laughed so much.

"I'm glad I could be there for you. I wish I'd been in Chicago with you, though. It's a really cool city. I could've shown you around." Linc lightly squeezed her fingers.

"I'm sure it's a fine city. I was in no mood to explore the city after they canceled my second day of interviews. Like, not at all."

"I guess." Linc changed the subject. "What does your week look like?"

"When do your friends get back?" Alexis wondered.

He picked up his phone. "If they aren't already back, they will be anytime."

Alexis tried to pull her hand away, but Linc wouldn't let go.

"What's going on in your head?"

She looked away. Linc followed her eyes as she gazed around the coffee shop. They had enjoyed the emptiness of the place throughout the week, but as if signaling the end of their alone time, retuning spring breakers flooded in.

Linc sat back in his chair. "That bad?"

"It's just been nice with all your friends several states away," she started, as she continued to avoid his eyes.

"They aren't that bad once you get to know them."

Alexis crossed her arms. "Do you even believe what you're saying?"

"I believe you're dodging my question."

"Classes and studying. Typical, college student agenda."

"Where am I on that agenda?"

Alexis' blank stare took him back to the first day he tried to talk to her.

"Come on. You think, now that my friends are back, my interest in you is going to disappear?" Linc released her hand, crossed his arms.

She sat silently for a moment, looked him in the eyes and said,

"I just figured your pursuit of charity would come to an end with their return."

"Not fair," he said quietly, pushing his chair back.

Alexis sat motionless.

A moment later, Linc switched seats to be closer to Alexis and took her chin in his hand to draw her close. "You really don't know much about men, do you?"

He leaned in to kiss her when a familiar and annoying voice broke Linc's concentration.

"O.M.F.G. You have got to be kidding me." Friendship Circle ambled up to their table. "I thought you were joking with this."

He pressed his lips gently against Alexis' for quick kiss.

"Nope," he responded, still staring into Alexis' eyes.

Come on, Pretty. Trust this.

They watched the overly tanned bleach blonde stalk away toward the door. "Disgusting," she mumbled loud enough to be heard by everyone in the general area.

Linc looked back to Alexis and gave a little tug on her hand. "So, when am I going to see you this week?"

"Ummmmm...really?"

Yeah.

Alexis sat back her chair and shifted the angle of her body away from Linc. "I don't know if that's a good idea now that–"

"Hey, my friends are going to love you. She's not one of my friends, so don't let her shittiness cloud what's happening here," Linc stated emphatically.

"We both know your friends are no better than she is."

Okay, that was a little harsh.

He wasn't giving up. "My friends are assholes. BUT, they are going to like you once they get to know you."

"Comforting."

"Please, don't give up on us. When am I going to get to spend time with you next week?"

"I'll be studying here most of the week. I guess you can join me if you'd like."

"AND..."

Alexis turned to face Linc. "What and?"

"And..." Linc brushed his lips against hers. "I want to see you outside of this coffee shop. Let's go out on Saturday. Dinner and a movie."

"Maybe."

"What maybe?" he replied, shocked.

"I'm not convinced this is going to work, now that they're back."

"It'll work. Better idea. Let's hang out at my place on Saturday, and I'll have everyone over to meet you. That way–"

Alexis threw up her hands, forcing Linc away. "Ummmm...NO!"

"What?"

A party is always a good idea.

There was fear in her eyes.

"Too soon."

"Okay. It's going to happen, so you need to prepare yourself. I know they didn't make the best first impression. They are good guys."

"Sure they are." Alexis gathered her books. "I should get going. I'm sure you want to catch up with your friends."

Linc grabbed Alexis' wrist. "They can wait."

"I have some things to do at home, so this is a good time."

"Can I, at the very least, drive you home?"

Linc released his hold, and Alexis tucked her booked away.

"Nah. I'll walk. Go see your friends. They'll be expecting you."

This isn't how this day was supposed to end.

He watched her for a moment. "Why does it feel like you're going to disappear once we leave here?"

Alexis' low volume, rapid-nervous sounding laugh caught Linc's attention. It was the first time he had heard her use it.

"We go to the same school. You know where I live. You know the only place I study. How can I disappear?"

"All solid points. I'd still like to make sure you get home safely."

"Linc, I've been getting to and from this coffee shop long before you and I met. I'll be fine."

"Alexis, that was before you had a boyfriend."

Alexis gasped.

He laughed at her stunned expression. "Speechless, I guess I'll head out. I'll text you later, or you could text me."

He stood, leaned over, kissed Alexis on the forehead, and

whispered in her ear before heading out the door, "Thanks for a great week. I'm looking forward to many more great weeks with you."

As the door closed behind him, Linc heard JoAnne say, "Girl, close your mouth and..."

CHAPTER 25

Dude, relax. This is going to go so much better than you have built it up. Worst case, they act like the assholes you know they are, and you have to kick their asses. Then, it's done.

Linc stood at the bottom step of Mikey's and Harrison's front porch, gripping a case of Rolling Rock.

"Alexis is worth all of this and more," Linc reminded himself and the universe as he slowly climbed the steps.

"Welcome home! Beers for all!" His voice rang through the house. He walked through a beautifully furnished home to the only room that was ever occupied, the game room.

Alexis' apartment would easily fit in here too. Damn. Puts it all in perspective. Okay, my friends, please don't be asshats.

Linc placed the beer on the table in front of his friends.

"This in no way makes up for you missing the trip," Harrison declared, without taking his eyes off the video game before him.

Linc popped a beer open and passed it to Mikey.

Mikey tossed the controller down. "We're squared up in my book."

Harrison paused the game and looked at Mikey. "Couldn't you have waited for the second case of beer before letting him off the hook?"

"There's only one case." Linc took a seat in the chair.

Harrison locked eyes with Linc, and then looked at the beer.

Get it yourself, asshole.

"Screw you." Harrison got up and grabbed a beer.

Mikey had restarted the game while Harrison was attempting to assert his dominance over Linc and killed his opponent.

"And, screw you too, Mikey," Harrison said, as he twisted the top off a bottle.

After two hours of beer drinking, playing video games, and sharing stories about their trip, Linc knew he had to tell his friends about Alexis. Before he could say anything, the theme song from *Friends* rang out.

Mikey spit out his sip of beer all over himself.

"What the hell?" Linc asked, bewildered as Harrison pulled his phone out of his pocket and walked out of the room to answer it.

"Explain," Linc demanded.

Mikey fell off the couch laughing and wiped the beer off his mouth and shirt with the takeout napkins that seemed to live on their coffee table. He tried to catch his breath.

"Speak."

He held up his hand. "Wait for this—"

Harrison stepped back into the room. "You fucked the cow."

"What?" Mikey asked, climbing back on the sofa and looking back and forth from Linc to Harrison.

That's the last time you'll call her that.

"Cow?" Linc asked.

His friends stared at him.

Harrison cleared his throat. "Are you seeing that fat piece of charity work from the coffee shop?"

Mikey's eyes grew bigger as he looked from Harrison to Linc.

Linc pulled the last beer out of the case and twisted the cap off. He tossed the cap back into the case where the others had collected. Linc tipped up the bottle and enjoyed a long pull.

"Alexis."

"What?" Mikey asked.

"Her name is Alexis. Make sure that's how you refer to her."

"What the fuck ever," Harrison said, as he headed into the other room.

Mikey waited until Harrison was in the kitchen. "Man, what the hell are you doing?"

How do you do this?

Linc ran his finger over the thirty-three on the back of the beer bottle. The theme song on the game repeated over and over. Mikey waited for Linc to explain.

"She's different," Linc started.

"She's huge!" Mikey corrected.

Linc sat the bottle on the coffee table. "She makes me feel different about things."

Mikey didn't say anything, but Linc felt him watching.

Come on, Dude. Tell him.

"I like her, Mikey."

Both guys sat in the silence of their thoughts.

Mikey held up his hands defensively. "Alexis?"

Linc nodded.

"Alexis is a lot of woman." His friend was trying, and Linc appreciated it. "She isn't someone I'd ever imagine you would be attracted to. You have tons of girls to choose from. Hell, Friendship Circle would step over any of us to get you in bed–"

"And..."

"And why settle for someone like her–no offense–when you can have someone more in your league?" Mikey inquired.

Linc shot out of his chair and paced behind the sofa. "Trust me, I'm not the one settling. If anything, Alexis is stepping down a peg to be with me. I had to convince her I was worth it, too."

"She's fucking FAT!" Harrison shouted, obviously listening from the other room.

Linc froze.

Mikey exhaled and sat back with his hands over his head.

"It's just unacceptable!" Harrison wailed. "You're the captain of the swim fucking team."

"And?" Linc and Mikey barked out in unison.

"It just doesn't work that way. A good-looking guy that works out and is fit can't be with a fat chick." Harrison dropped into his spot on the sofa. "This is not news. Everyone knows this."

Just get the hell out of here.

"I'm out." Linc moved for the door.

"Linc, let's talk this out." Mikey played the sensible one of the group.

"Mike, there's nothing to work out. My girlfriend's name is Alexis. You'll show her the respect she deserves, or –"

"Or, what?" Harrison pushed.

"Or, stay away from us." Linc's cold tone left no room for debate.

Phone in hand, Linc had the text screen up before his foot hit the last step. There were only two people he wanted to talk to after that run in, his sister and Alexis.

Linc: I need to talk.

L: Did boyfriend freak you out?

CHAPTER 26

"Hello?"

"Sorry! You needed me." Grace said, almost shouting. "I had to fly to Uganda to check on the project. I'm just now getting all my texts."

Linc rubbed his eyes and propped himself up on the pillows. "Is everything okay?"

"Yeah, fine. Were you in the pool?"

"No. I was sleeping," Linc replied. He paused for an overhead speaker in Grace's background to finish. "Where are you?"

"Train station. I only have a few minutes before my train departs." Grace spoke faster than normal. "You said you needed to talk, so what's wrong?"

"Why does something have to be wrong for me to want to talk to my sister? I miss you, that's all." Linc stared at the poster of the Golden Gate Bridge and San Francisco's skyline.

"Minutes, HL. My train leaves in minutes. Spill."

In quiet voice, Linc shared, "It was about Alexis."

"Was?"

"My friends freaked out when they found out."

"Why?"

"Her size."

"And your friends are assholes."

"It's more than that, Grace. I don't know how she does it. We were at the zoo, and she just smiled through strangers making shitty comments about her weight."

"Well, she's lives in her skin every day. I can't imagine what she goes through."

"It sucks."

"The hard part for you may be figuring out if you're willing to deal with it too."

"I am. I told Mikey and Harrison if they couldn't respect her, they needed to stay away from us."

"Sounds like she's pretty special. I'm looking forward to meeting her."

"Wait, what?"

"They've called my train. Gotta run."

"Grace!"

"I'm coming home. Talk soon. Most."

The noise of the hustle and bustle surrounding his sister went silent. Grace was on her way to another exciting destination. And, once again, she didn't share any details of her trip. But, then, that wasn't unusual.

Shit. When?

Linc slid down onto his pillow. He closed his eyes. Thoughts of the most important person in his life meeting Alexis kept him from falling back to sleep. He decided to wait to tell Alexis about Grace's return until he had all the details.

Church bells rang.

"Hi, Mom," Linc answered sleepily. He wanted to ask his mom when Grace was coming home but they had made an agreement a long time ago. Neither Grace nor Linc would share with their mother the fact that they had spoken to each other. They had each witnessed her use the other's words against them, and it had resulted in a pact being formed. Both were confident their dad was aware of the pact.

"What's wrong?" his mother questioned suspiciously.

"Nothing."

She didn't miss a beat. "Why aren't you at the pool?"

"Season's over, Mom." Linc rolled his eyes as he spoke.

A pause expanded between them.

His mother broke the silence. "Herbert Lincoln James, are you telling me you're done with swimming?" The excitement in her voice was unmistakable. Linc could almost taste the calculations churning about how her son could better spend his time to further his future.

"Mother, stop. Yes, the season is over. I'm not in training mode. Swimming will always be something I do."

His mother did what she had always done. She ignored him. "I have news."

The tone was a familiar one. This was not going to be about

Grace coming home.

"I ran into Representative McCloud at the club. He asked if you were available to work in his office over the summer."

Years of experience had taught Linc to just listen to his mom when she started down the path of politics.

"Lincoln, did you hear me?" The annoyance was clear.

"Yes, Mom," Linc replied. He heard her inhale the large breath of air needed to state her case and slipped in, "Mom, I'm going to be late. I've–"

"Hurry. You cannot be late. You know that."

Linc laid his phone down. His mother's obsession with punctuality was a useful tool for escaping unpleasant conversations. Her need to always appear in control and poised required every family member to be no less then fifteen minutes early to any scheduled meeting.

She skipped over telling you Grace is coming home. Unbelievable.

Before heading to the kitchen, Linc sent his sister an email telling her how excited he was about her coming home and attached one of the many pictures he had taken of Gage at the shelter explaining he would be a great dog for her. The thought of being able to introduce Alexis to Grace brought a smile to his face. It also erased the conversation he'd just had with his mother.

...

Highway driving had always been relaxing for Linc. He weaved in and out of traffic while the details of the various meetings churned in his head.

Music played. Sights were occasionally pointed out. Alexis laid her head back and closed her eyes at one point, prompting Linc to place his hand on her thigh. When she opened her eyes, he smiled and squeezed her leg before once again getting lost in the thoughts running rampant through his head.

Unlike the trip to the zoo, Linc turned the music up loud and talking was at a minimum, though it was doubtful either would be able to name one song that had played in the two-hour drive.

At their destination, Linc reached for Alexis' hand and led her slowly to the wooded boardwalk that ran in front of Lake Michigan. During the car ride to the zoo, Alexis mentioned Lake

Michigan being one of her favorite places, and not being able to recall the last time she and her family had visited. Linc had looked forward to surprising her with the destination all week.

"I had a busy couple of days," Linc blurted out.

"I wondered." Alexis tightened her fingers around his. "Is everything okay?"

"I interviewed for another teaching position."

Alexis listened.

"I'd be teaching ninth and tenth graders. This school doesn't have a swim team but the kids and their parents have been asking for a program." He finished and stared out at the water.

"And the idea of starting from nothing and being able to build it up is intriguing to you?" Alexis asked knowingly.

Linc nodded his head. "Yes."

Alexis continued to probe. "But, you still don't know if you're ready to give up competitive swimming."

Linc watched the whitecaps roll up and crash onshore. Almost lost in the repetition of the waves, his thoughts wrestled to make sense. "The pool has been my life since I started swimming. People know me as a swimmer first and everything else after. Shit, I don't even know what the other stuff is."

Alexis waited.

"My sister and mom both called me this morning and wondered why I wasn't in the pool. I wondered why I wasn't in the pool, too. How can I even think about walking away from being on the pool deck every day?"

"Why weren't you at the pool this morning?"

Linc walked over to one of the many benches built into the walkway every few yards. "Sit with me?"

Alexis joined him, but remained quiet.

He gazed at her long brown hair that had been on top of her head in a messy bun on the day he had first seen her. It now blew freely in the wind, the sun releasing all the hidden secrets of red highlights mixed in with the different shades of brown. Linc watched her eyes dance as she waited patiently for whatever he was prepared to share.

You. You're changing everything.

"I haven't felt that pull to be in the pool. At least, not in the same way. I'm not making sense. You've made me feel different.

You've made everything different."

Alexis bolted from her seat, stepped off the walkway into the thick sand, and headed for the water's edge. Surprised, Linc had no choice but to go after her.

Okay, what the hell just happened?

"Too honest?" Linc asked, as he joined her where she stood in the sand.

Alexis was breathing deeply. "I..."

A wave crashed at their feet, and water rushed up to the edges of their shoes.

She opened her mouth and closed it, rolled her eyes away to the sky, and then looked down at her feet. "I don't want to make things complicated for you. I don't know how to do this right. I've never–"

"I know this is new for you." Linc took her hand and squeezed it. "We can learn together. Okay?"

Alexis gently extracted her hand from Linc's and hugged him. Barely a whisper over the sound of the water, he heard in his ear, "Thank you."

CHAPTER 27

Linc sat focused on his phone. The sound of JoAnne clearing her throat startled him. He fumbled his phone and it hit the table with a thud.

She slid into the seat next to him. "Linc, I'm so sorry. Is it broken?"

"No, but, shit, you scared me." He examined the phone, but knew it would be fine.

"Where's Alexis?" JoAnne wondered.

Just the sound of her name made Linc smile. He sat back and found an equally big smile on JoAnne's face. "She's on her way. Need something?"

JoAnne nodded and pointed to her co-worker. "I need to find an excuse to get out of this shift tonight. You're looking happy, so I'm sure you're not covering for me."

"I just learned how to order correctly, so I'm not sure they're going to let me make the coffees. Hot date?" Linc thought JoAnne worked too much since Alexis told him she was in school.

"I won tickets to tonight's Daughtry concert on the radio today." She threw her hands in the air. "None of my wonderful co-workers will cover for me."

"You kind of look like you don't feel good to me." Linc winked. "Are you sure you're well enough to work around food tonight?"

Alexis entered the coffee shop, smiled and signaled she'd be right there. Linc enjoyed every step she took toward the restroom.

JoAnne waved her hands in front of him. "Did you hear anything I said?"

Linc shook his head.

"You're so whipped," JoAnne said.

With a grin, he instructed, "Repeat, please."

"I said I'm not going to sneak around to go to a concert. My responsibility is to my job." She gritted her teeth and made a fist. "Of course, I would win on a night I have to work."

Linc felt badly. "I wish I could help."

"Thanks, me too." JoAnne thought for a minute. "Hey, why don't the two of you use the tickets? At least they wouldn't be wasted."

"Oh, I don't know."

"You don't know what?" Alexis asked, as she reached her seat.

"Go see Daughtry. I won tickets for the concert tonight in Grand Rapids, but I have to work," JoAnne said with muted happiness.

"Who?"

"Alexis, come on. Daughtry. Idol. The greatest TV show in the history of TV. You know. Simon Cowell."

"Simon who? Idol what?"

JoAnne threw her hands in the air. "Are you joking–"

"Excuse me, Ladies." Linc walked to the counter leaving JoAnne and Alexis to all things Simon Cowell.

"May I help you?" Rachel asked. She was a barista Linc had only interacted with a couple of times.

"I have a proposition for you." Linc said, with a quick glance back at the table to see if either of the girls were watching. Rachel eyed him with curiosity and skepticism. "How would you like to make a quick fifty bucks?"

She leaned against the counter and inclined her head toward Linc. "How?"

He removed his wallet from his back pocket and looked inside. "Actually, I have a hundred dollars on me that could all be yours." He took the money from his wallet and spread the bills to show the barista.

Her smile faded. "What do I have to do?"

"Tell JoAnne you'll work for her so she can take the night off."

"And?" she said suspiciously.

"And you can't tell her I'm paying you to do it. You have to convince her it's all your idea." He looked over his shoulder again. The girls were deep in conversation.

"You're saying if I volunteer to take her shift and make it seem like it was my idea, you'll give me a hundred bucks?" Rachel waited for Linc to respond.

"Make a couple of vanilla lattes for me to take back to the table, and we have a deal."

The girl whipped the coffees together without another word. She even offered him a cookie, but he declined.

As he picked up the coffees from the counter, Rachel ran around the counter to the table where JoAnne and Alexis were talking.

"Excuse me?" she interrupted them.

Linc strolled over and placed a coffee in front of Alexis. He bent and kissed her cheek, causing her to smile. JoAnne watched their interaction like she was the proud parent to both.

"JoAnne, my plans got canceled for tonight. If you still wanted me to work for you–"

"What?!" JoAnne screeched. "Are you serious?"

"Yep. I can close–"

JoAnne jumped up out of her chair and hugged the girl. "Thank you so much, Rachel!"

Well done.

"Oh." Her happiness fell away. The tickets were in Alexis' hand. "That's okay. I already gave the tickets to them."

"Oh, no, you didn't! I don't want to sit through Daughtry." Alexis eagerly handed the tickets back to her friend.

"OMG! OMG! OMG! I'm going to see my favorite Idol, Daughtry!" JoAnne hopped around the table.

"Shouldn't you get going, JoAnne?" Rachel glanced at Linc. "It's a drive, and you want to be able to look at the merch table."

"I'm out! Thanks again, Rachel." JoAnne waved to everyone and was out the door like a shot.

Alexis laughed. "I guess we weren't meant to go to the concert tonight. That was really cool of you, Rachel."

Rachel remained standing at the table.

"I'm nothing, if not cool," she said, directly to Linc.

Customers entered the coffee shop, but Rachel ignored them and remained planted in her spot.

Linc pulled out his wallet and handed her all his cash. Without a word, she pivoted, walked around the counter, and began taking orders and making coffee.

"You paid her to cover for JoAnne?"

Linc nodded.

"Why?"

"JoAnne's your friend," he answered.

For you.

Alexis blew him a kiss. "Thank you. That was very kind."

For that.

"Since I'm in your good graces at the moment, this seems like the perfect time to talk about meeting my friends." He wouldn't let go of Alexis's hand when she tried to pull away. "Just a minute. They all want to meet you."

Alexis rolled her eyes. "Yeah, right. They want to meet me."

She tugged at her hand again, and Linc released his hold.

"How about we start with two of my friends so it's less..." Linc searched for the right word.

Alexis knew exactly what it was. "Terrifying."

She crossed her arms and stared at her coffee cup, avoiding eye contact.

"Perhaps, overwhelming, but we can use your word," Linc joked, but Alexis didn't laughed. "Please, one night at my place."

"Fine. But, if I get uncomfortable I'm out."

Linc smiled. "It'll be fine."

"And, you promise to let me leave."

"Deal."

It's going to be fine. I'll kill them if they aren't on their best behavior."

CHAPTER 28

Linc proudly sat in his seat, beating his friends at their own video game. He smiled at himself.

"Shit, your girl can cook her ass off," Mikey said, as he tried to push the buttons all the way through the controller. "I've never even heard of white lasagna."

See, this is going to work. Everything is fine.

Harrison had eaten three helpings of the dinner Alexis had prepared for his friends. Watching her relax had been the best part of dinner. Mikey and Harrison had grilled her with questions about basketball teams and Spartan football. His girl had held her own. Everyone had laughed.

You should be helping her with the dishes. She insisted on doing it herself. This is going to be the first of many–

Knock. Knock. Knock.

"Mikey." Linc gestured toward the door.

Mikey was up, had opened the door, and was back in his seat with controller in hand in record time. Friendship Circle entered wearing another barely there dress. She closed the door behind her.

What the hell are you doing here? SHIT!!!

"What are you doing here?" Linc asked.

She walked over and stood in front of him. "Just checking to see if you've come to your senses yet. We can get back to where we were."

"This should get interesting. Charity is going to be pissed!" Harrison joked.

Alexis gasped, and everyone turned to find Alexis framed by the light from the kitchen. In slow motion, she grabbed her purse and headed for the door.

Linc froze.

Shit!

The guys looked at him.

Friendship Circle started to laugh.

"LINC!" Mikey barked, propelling Linc to the door.

As the door closed behind him, Linc heard Harrison and Friendship Circle laughing and Mikey yell, "SHIT!"

Alexis was to the end of the walkway.

"STOP!"

She turned and waited for him to reach her. Words left her mouth like bullets. "So, they call me Charity?"

"They know how I feel about you and that it pisses me off."

Alexis' death stare was overwhelming.

"Yes, Harrison does," he admitted.

She took a step back, and the death stare transformed into disgust. Linc reached for her.

"Don't," she commanded.

Shit.

Alexis spun and walked away from him.

Shit.

He took two steps to follow her, but she threw up her hand and said, "Don't even."

Linc watched her turn the corner. It had been Alexis that had shown the charity. Over and over again, he had put her in positions that could hurt her, yet she had continued to spend time with him. 'Trust me,' he had convinced her, but he had failed her.

As he walked back into his house, Linc overheard Harrison say, "...the last time I paid attention to the color on the fingernails wrapped around my dick? Never."

"You! Get out now!" Linc was pointing at Friendship Circle. "Do not come back to this house, ever. Do not speak to me. Do not say my name. Do not speak to Alexis. Got it?"

"What did I do?" she asked, stunned.

Linc's voice grew louder. "Leave now!"

Harrison started laughing. "Come on, man. Chill out."

Mikey tapped Harrison's arm and shook his head.

"What?"

Mikey held up both hands in exasperation.

"You shut the fuck up, and we can talk in a minute. Or leave with her." Linc's tone was unyielding.

Friendship Circle started, "Linc, I–"

"I have asked you to leave. You are trespassing. I'm calling the police." Linc's voice echoed the same crisp, clear, biting voice Alexis had just used on him.

"I'm leaving. Just so you know, everyone is making fun of you and your fat cow of a girlfriend. It's embarrassing."

"OUT!" he yelled.

Slowly, Friendship Circle rose from her perch on the couch next to Harrison and walked out the door.

Linc slammed it behind her.

"You!" He pointed to Harrison. "You call my girl Charity one more time, and you and me are going to have a serious problem. Am I clear?"

"Linc, it's just a joke. I don't mean anything by it, and you know it." Harrison picked up the controller and pressed play.

Linc took a step toward his friend, but Mikey chimed in before a fight could break out. "Harrison, it's an asshole move, and you know it. She's Linc's girl. End of story. Show your teammate some respect. Shit, show Alexis some respect."

Harrison paused the game and looked at Mikey. "Are you serious right now with this?"

"Yeah, man. I'm totally serious. Stop being a prick."

"Harrison, I'm not going to allow a repeat of this to happen. Alexis means too much to me."

"Let me get this straight. You're calling me out?" Harrison asked.

"No more calling Alexis 'Charity.' Got it?" Linc repeated to the biting tone that had worked so well up to this point.

Harrison threw the controller at the coffee table and got up.

"I cannot believe you're choosing her over me. Yeah, I understand, no more Charity."

He walked out and firmly pulled the door closed.

Mikey picked up the controller and started a new game.

"You have anything to say?" Linc inquired.

Mikey paused the game. "Crackers love cheese."

The room was silent for a moment while Linc gave Mikey a blank stare. Mikey's eyebrow lifted, and Linc smirked, then they started laughing. Mikey pressed a button, and the game started.

"Alexis okay?" Mikey asked.

"She's pissed as hell at me."

Mikey killed Linc's avatar, then he tossed the controller on the coffee table and got to his feet. "Well, you let your friend make fun of your girl. You let some chick who clearly has no respect for your relationship, or your girl, come over to your place, and you're sitting here playing a video game with me."

Before Linc could defend himself, Mikey continued. "You're either a shitty boyfriend or you don't really give a fuck about her. Either way, yeah, I can see why she's pissed."

Mikey walked out the door.

Dude, you suck.

CHAPTER 29

Linc waited in the car until he saw JoAnne come from behind the counter. She came to the door and began spraying it with cleaner on the window. He got out of the car and sulked toward her.

"Is she here?" he asked, as JoAnne opened the door for him.

"Nope, she left a few minutes ago."

Linc turned to return to his car.

"She's not going home yet."

His entire body slumped.

JoAnne touched his back. "Come on. Let's have some tea."

Jeez, it's that bad.

"I messed up."

"Yep, and your friends are all total assholes," JoAnne added, as she made her way behind the counter.

The tone of a text alert sounded on Linc's phone. His heart banged in his chest as he reached for it.

Please be Alexis.

Grace: Word of the day...aginner.

"From my sister," he said. "I was hoping it was Al–"

His phone started playing church bells.

Excellent, because you're day isn't going bad enough.

"Hello?"

"Herbert Lincoln James!" His mother shouted into the phone. "Have you been in public with a fat girl?"

JoAnne's eyes got huge as she set two cups of tea on the table.

"I–"

There was no way he was getting in anything during this conversation.

"Do. You. Know. What. People. Will. Think?"

"It's–"

"I did not work this hard to give you everything you've ever wanted so you could throw your reputation away with some fat person. How many times have I told you that image is everything? You are a star athlete. You are your father's son. You are going to be in the public eye for the rest of your life."

"Mother, she's a–"

"Cow. Pig. Embarrassment."

He listened to her pause to take a drink.

This is not the time to deal with this. Stay calm and get her off the phone.

"You have an expectation to live up to, and it cannot be done spending time with some huge, ugly girl that cannot sit in a chair comfortably. Am I clear?"

She's beautiful. She's a Kennedy. She made life simpler. And, I'm falling for her.

He touched the rim of the teacup placed before him.

"Lincoln, am I clear? Do I need to express my feelings directly to this woman?"

"NO!"

"Then this is settled." His mother waited silently for his response.

"Yes," Linc said, saying anything to get his tipsy mother off the subject and off the phone.

"Good. Now, your father and I will be there for graduation. We'll need to meet in Novi next weekend to shop for a decent suit."

"I'm not wearing a suit for graduation. I have to go."

His mom, in the most delightful voice, told her son they would talk in a couple of days. He disconnected without saying bye.

Linc and JoAnne sat silently after he lowered his phone to the table.

Rachel strolled up to the table and sat down. "Oh, hilarious. You're here now. JoAnne had the best time at the concert. Did she tell you?"

JoAnne nodded. "It was an amazing concert."

Linc nodded.

"Rachel, I can finish closing if you want to head out," JoAnne offered. Linc stared in appreciation.

"Okay by me. Though, I kind of want to hear how you're going to handle this one. You did so well with the last one, Dr. Phil."

JoAnne glared at Rachel.

"I was Dr. Ruth." Rachel said to Linc, as she walked toward the counter.

Linc took a sip of his tea and grimaced. "This is horrible."

JoAnne raised her cup toward her lips. "It's supposed to be bad. Helps make you forget what's bothering you."

He ran his finger over the rim of the cup. "This soil-tasting beverage is not going to make me forget that I messed up with Alexis."

"She has something better than tea for you." Rachel stated as she placed a to-go cup filled coffee on the table in front of him.

JoAnne hit Rachel's arm. "Go home."

"I'm going. I'm going."

"Thanks for this." Linc raised the coffee to his lips but returned it to the table when he felt the heat rippling off. "Hot."

"Double cup." JoAnne winked at Linc and waved to Rachel as she left.

Linc waited for the door to swing shut.

"So, you know what happened?" When JoAnne nodded, he continued. "I shouldn't have let her leave."

JoAnne smacked the table. "You shouldn't let your asshole friends, and some girl that wants to sleep with you, around Alexis."

Linc winced.

"Her feelings are hurt. Can you blame her for leaving?" JoAnne paused. "Charity?"

Linc held his hands up in defense. "I know. I've talked to my friends. They are slow picking up on how much I like Alexis."

The phone vibrated against the table. Linc read the text.

Alexis: We need to talk. How about dinner on Sunday?

Yes! Wait, we need to talk. Sunday. That's two days away.

He looked at JoAnne, searching for anything to hold on to. She stared back.

"Is she going to break up with me?" he asked quietly.

JoAnne shrugged, "Alexis tends to act unexpectedly. Never would I have thought she would agree to date you. But she did. Anything could happen."

Shit, she is totally going to end this.

"Great." Linc leaned back onto the back legs of the chair. "I'm so glad everyone is in my corner with her."

JoAnne stood. "I thought I was clear on day one. I'm on Alexis' side." JoAnne picked up both teacups. "You hurt her. You're very lucky I haven't kicked you in the balls and sent you on your way."

The chair legs hit the floor with a thud.

"Okay, I guess I'm ahead." Linc leaned forward and placed his arms on the table, balls safely out of the way. "JoAnne, I'm going fix this."

"You better."

CHAPTER 30

"Door is open...come in," Alexis yelled, from inside her apartment.

Okay. She doesn't sound like she's breaking up with you.

Linc pushed the door open. The shades had been drawn, and the lack of light surprised him.

So, this is new.

A cluster of candles in the seating area, and a few more scattered around the apartment, illuminated the space. As he adjusted to the glow, his eyes stopped on Alexis' futon. It was laid flat and had a white fluffy looking comforter.

Now that's super new.

"So, Alexis. I'm here." He heard the shaking in his own voice.

"I'll be right out. There's wine chilling. If you want to open it, go ahead," Alexis replied, through the bathroom door.

Wine?

"I'm good. Thanks."

"Okay."

"Are we going..."

Alexis walked out of the bathroom.

Linc blinked. Twice.

Alexis stood in a long, pink, silky nightgown.

Definitely not going out.

"Wow. You look–" Linc fumbled for the right words. "You look really good. Your hair is...WOW."

Alexis stood looking at him. Even in the glow of the candles, Linc could tell she was struggling with something. There was a smile on her face but her hands were locked in front of her body as if she were trying to show a certain angle.

"You're lovely," he whispered.

Grrrrr. Be her friend.

Linc had meant for the comment to stay in his thoughts, but it slipped out as Alexis shifted her weight from one foot to the other.

"Thank you," she returned in a hushed voice.

"So, no dinner out, I take it."

She giggled. It wasn't her normal laugh. This one was higher, forced. "I thought we could stay in and talk."

Yeah, right. With her wearing that.

As she approached, the silkiness of the gown displayed her breasts like a billboard on the side of a highway. They couldn't be missed.

Stop looking. Dude, you want to touch her. You know you want to press your entire body up against her and experience how the silkiness feels. DUDE!! Back it down.

Alexis sat and gestured. "Sit, please."

Linc lowered himself into the chair facing the cloud-like bed.

As your hand enters the water, angle it to maximize the cut of your stroke.

"Are you sure you don't want any wine? I guess I should have gotten beer. I know you like beer." Alexis stared at the wine bottle and wine glasses.

"I'm good. I don't really feel much like drinking tonight. It isn't worth the risk of driving home drunk."

"You could stay," Alexis volunteered, bashfully.

WOW...Didn't see that one coming? Should have. Didn't. Shit!! This is not a good idea. Lincoln, she hasn't talked to you for a couple of days, and now this. Come on, Dude. BE HER FRIEND!

"What are we doing for dinner? I am starving. I wasn't supposed to pick something up, was I?"

"No. It should be here—"

A knock at the door interrupted Alexis mid-sentence. She moved towards the door.

You are not opening the door looking like that.

She reached for a pink, black, and white silky robe next to the door. Wrapping it around herself, she opened the door.

Linc exhaled the breath he'd been holding.

Alexis closed the door and turned with two large bags. She shrugged out of the robe while she maneuvered the bags and left it where it fell to the floor, then placed the bags on the small table next to Linc's chair.

"Dinner is served."

The familiar smile returned to Alexis' face as she unpacked the bags. She grabbed two water bottles out of the mini fridge and set them next to the containers.

"Spaghetti?"

Alexis nodded.

"From–"

No, she didn't.

"Yep."

"Rotunno's? I didn't know they delivered. This is so cool."

The two sat and ate in near silence. Linc wondered if she could hear his thoughts. He smiled when she looked at him.

Why not ask her? OMG, the strap is falling. Shit!! She looks so hot.

Alexis pushed the thin strap back into place. Linc followed fingers as they slowly trailed down her arm. His entire body vibrated.

Oh, this is going to be very difficult.

"They don't deliver. Someone owed me." She said, with a smirk on her face.

"Nice."

Silence blanketed the room again.

Dude, say something. Talk. Take it slow. I want to explore the universe of Alexis. Okay, don't say anything.

"Bread?"

"Thanks, I'm good," he replied. He took another huge bite of his favorite Italian dish from his favorite Italian restaurant.

"Actually, I'm asking if I could have the bread. It's in the bag next to you."

"Oh shit, yeah."

He handed Alexis the bag.

"What are you thinking about so deeply over there?" she inquired.

"You," Linc answered without hesitation.

Alexis nodded. He stared at her until she returned his look.

Linc risked it. "I love your smile."

She diverted her eyes to her dinner. Her hair cascaded down over her shoulder and chest when she tilted her head to the side.

Setting his container on the floor next to him, Linc took the two steps to Alexis and brushed her hair back. "No hiding your face with your hair. I want to see you."

Alexis gifted him with a blush as he slowly stepped backward to his seat. In the candlelight, she looked stunning.

Dude, you've got it bad.

"Anything new since we last spoke?"

Alexis froze.

She stopped mid-bite, looking past him, and shook her head no.

So, something is going on, but she isn't ready to talk about it.

He changed the subject. "I've missed you."

"I've missed you too." She took a bite. "It felt weird not talking to you these last two days."

"I tried to call you," he said. "I even came over here."

"I know. I needed to deal with what happened. Your friends are dicks, and I really don't ever need to see that woman again."

We've moved from assholes to dicks. I'm not sure, but this may be progress.

"Yes. And I couldn't agree with you more. I'm sorry."

Alexis nodded.

When the food was gone, Alexis gathered the containers and bagged them. The silkiness of her gown highlighted her curves, and as she bent over, it was clear she was naked underneath.

OMG...her ass. Feet together. Always keep your feet together. Hands–

"Excuse me, I'll be right back." Alexis quickly walked into the bathroom and closed the door.

Linc jumped to his feet to adjust himself.

Water...Her nipples were starting to harden. Swimming lanes...Her skin looked so soft as she brought the strap back onto her shoulder. Starting block...You want to know how she feels. Diving into the pool...Come on, Linc. Don't screw this up. GO SLOW. Not touching the wall...novice mistake.

He checked his phone. No message. No missed calls.

No way thinking about swimming is going to be enough.

The bathroom door opened. Alexis walked out slowly and kept her eyes on his.

FUCK!

The gown had gotten shorter. It was the same color and same silky material. Linc swallowed. His eyes traveled the entire length of the woman standing in front of him.

"I...I like your new outfit," was all he could manage.

"Do you? I didn't know if it was too much?" Alexis swayed back and forth, lifting the already short dress up her thigh. Careful not to look at Linc, Alexis took the last few steps to erase the distance between them.

"Not too much," Linc said slowly.

Standing in his personal space, Alexis placed her hands on her hips.

"We've finished dinner, and I don't own a TV. What would you like to do now?" she asked.

"I...I–"

Alexis poked fun at Linc. "You. You."

Nervous laughter escaped him.

Shit, not now. Water. Swim lanes. Hands. Dolphin kick.

"Do you want to go swimming?" Linc blurted out of nowhere.

"Swimming?" Alexis asked. She tilted her head to get a better look at his face.

"I'm not sure where that came from."

"Are you nervous?"

"So, yeah. I'm a little nervous."

Linc watched her lay down on her bed in what felt like slow motion. Alexis searched his eyes for something.

"Why?" she asked.

He knew exactly what she was asking. "Why, what?"

"Why are you still standing over there when I'm lying here all alone."

Okay, you totally didn't know what she was talking about.

In one large step, Linc was next to the bed and looking down at Alexis.

"No reason."

Shit. This is not good. You really want her.

"Do you require a written invitation?"

Linc's entire body woke up as he lay down on his stomach next to her. No amount of swimming words was going to distract him. He crossed his arms under his chin. Alexis filled his view. Her hair fell in big curly waves and spread across one of the pillows as if someone had spent time arranging it perfectly.

"Hi," she said, in the sultry tone that so many other girls had attempted and failed.

"What's up, Pretty?"

Alexis wrinkled her nose and smiled. "You're the first and only person to ever call me that," she said softly.

"I guess that makes me special."

"Or blind," she said.

"Hold on. Don't piss me off by saying negative things about my girl."

Alexis raised her head until their lips were centimeters apart. "Thank you, Linc."

He leaned in and brushed her lips with his. The air was cool and minty. Linc pulled away, but she leaned in.

Two quick pecks and he moved his head back to look into her eyes. Alexis' long lashes slowly parted and revealed her soft brown eyes. Trying to have a rational thought while this close to her body was impossible.

Just go for it. You both want it.

She leaned in and met him again, but this time her lips had parted so Linc could explore. The kiss deepened as he slid his tongue between her lips and across her tongue. Alexis moaned.

He pulled back again. "Can I use your bathroom?"

Alexis ran her fingers over her lips. "Yeah."

Water...shit, her smile. Swimming lane...shit, her lips are so soft. Starting block...shit, her nails on the back of my neck. Diving into the pool...shit, she smells so damn good. Dolphin...Shit, she's going to feel so good. DUDE, STOP!! Big picture this moment for a second.

Linc jumped off the bed, and looked at Alexis.

"What's wrong?" she asked confused.

"Nothing. I just don't want to rush this."

"So, touching me is rushing?"

"Alexis."

"Seriously."

"Come on. I've had sex with a lot of women and I don't want–"

"Exactly. You don't want."

"Are you going to let me finish?"

"Finish? You don't even want to start. You haven't wanted to start since ever."

Her words caught him off guard. "Wait, what?"

"Nothing."

Linc scrambled. "Hold on."

"Why?"

"You think this is because I don't want you?"

"I think you would've already fucked what's-her-name and all the others. But me, you barely want to kiss."

"Alexis, we're different."

She covered herself with a blanket. "Oh, I get that."

"You're different than they are."

"Clearly!"

"No, that's not what I mean." Nothing he said was working. "This isn't coming out right at all."

"Just go," Alexis whispered.

"What? No!"

"I don't want to talk anymore."

WHAT THE FUCK IS HAPPENING!

"We haven't even begun to talk. You need to understand something," he said.

"I understand something just fine."

"Alexis, let me explain."

"What? That I'm 'special?' That I'm not like the others?"

"Exactly."

"Linc, I'm just a girl that likes you a lot. I thought you liked me too. I thought you wanted to be with me."

Linc looked away to organize his thoughts.

"I like you in a different way than I liked the others."

"Get out," Alexis cried.

He had never seen so much distress in her. Not when his friends called her, Charity. Not when strangers called her hurtful things at the zoo. Not even when Friendship Circle had laughed at her. This was a pain that only he had the ability to cause.

Linc wanted to climb back on the bed and hold her. Comfort her.

He took one step toward her.

"No. I don't want your charity anymore."

"That is not what this is. I didn't explain it right."

"Actually, you explained it really well. I'm different than all the other girls you've been with. All the others you chose to be physical with. All the others you couldn't keep your hands off. I totally get it. I'm special."

"WOW...you are totally twisting my words."

"Am I? Answer me this question, then. Why haven't we had sex yet? Hell, why haven't we really even messed around?"

He answered honestly, without thought, "Because I feel differently about you."

"Yeah, well I don't want to be with a guy that feels so differently about me that he doesn't want to touch me."

"OMG. Stop it! I like you, okay? Alexis, I like you."

"So what's the problem, then?" she asked. "Why won't you touch me?"

"I want to take this slowly. I don't want to rush it."

"That doesn't even make sense."

Linc shrugged.

"Just go," she begged.

"Are you serious?"

"Yes."

"You want me to leave, really?"

Alexis nodded as she cried.

"I don't want to leave you alone when you're upset."

"The choice isn't yours. Go."

Linc took another step in her direction. He was close enough to touch her shoulder. Caress her hair. He wanted to wipe her tears away, but she hid her face from him. Aching and uncertain, he stood listening to her soft cries.

Come on, explain it better. Make her understand. She means more to you than the rest. You want a relationship with her, not just sex. Tell her sex always ruins it with you. Dude, don't walk out of here with her this upset.

"Alexis, can I–"

"No. Just leave." And, in a whisper, she added, "Please."

Linc couldn't release the handle on her door. He stood there like an idiot, unable to let go.

Dude, what if you let go and it's the end for the two of you? Come on, Man. Let go. Call her tomorrow and explain.

That's when it happened.

He heard her sobbing. Not crying. Not like girls cry at movies. Sobbing. The agony of deep hurt, of someone who didn't have any other choice but to release it through a flood of tears.

Let her have her space, Asshole. You've done enough for one day.

    Linc let go of the knob.

CHAPTER 31

Back at his house, Linc walked to the kitchen and opened a bottle of Jack Daniels. He grabbed a six-pack out of the refrigerator and carried his haul to the dark living room to sit in his spot and replay what had transpired. He took a long swig of the Jack, then propped the bottle between his legs so he could snap the cap off the first beer. He hurled the bit of metal across the room.

How the hell did this happen?

He replayed her words.

"Yeah, well I don't want to be with a guy that feels so differently about me that he doesn't want to touch me."

How are you going to fix this one?

Another swig of Jack was followed by another pull of the beer.

Seriously. Dude, you finally find a woman that's special, that you don't want to just fall into bed with, and you're kicked out of her apartment.

Another swig of Jack. More beer.

"And, by the way, Alexis Kennedy Hewson, do you think it was easy for me to stop when I did? Hell, no. I wanted to explore every part of you." Linc's voice rang loud in the quiet, pitch-black room.

Another swig of Jack. More beer.

Inside and out. Hell, yeah.

"Man, you're so soft. Your lips are like perfection. And you smell so damn good. I don't know how you always smell so good, but it drives me crazy."

Another swig. Another beer.

"So, the answer is no. It wasn't easy for me to leave you laying there all silky soft and smelling good in that bed. Do I get any credit for that?"

Another swig. More beer.

"Nope. No credit. In fact, quite the opposite, actually. You throw me out of your cute, tiny apartment. An apartment that smells just like you," Linc yelled into the emptiness.

Another swig of Jack.

And my beer is gone.

Linc tried to stand with bottles in both hands. Halfway off the sofa, he lost his balance and reached for the armrest for support. The empty beer bottle flew to the floor between the side table and the sofa.

Ha. Alexis Kennedy Hewson every damn one of your smiles keeps my world off-balance in the best way ever.

"I might be gettin' drunk, though."

Placing the Jack bottle on the coffee table, Linc used both hands to walk up the back of the sofa to a standing position. He took a step toward the kitchen and fell forward into the lamp, knocking it off the side table, and breaking it into several pieces.

"I'm messing up everywhere today."

You're drunk.

Linc took two extra steps to the right, then corrected himself by stepping to the left, and finally ended up in front of the refrigerator. With fresh bottles of beer in each hand, he wobbled back to the sofa.

Damn, you are so complicated. What the hell do you want done to prove that...

"SHIT!"

Setting all the bottles on the coffee table in front of him, his face planted into his hands.

Shit! You're an idiot! She needed to know you wanted her. Shit!

"Well, this isn't good at all."

Reaching for his phone, Linc scrolled to her name.

"I love this picture," he announced, and showed the empty room.

While they were on their zoo date, Linc had taken the picture without Alexis knowing it. She had been standing at the glass wall, and a sea otter had been playing in front of her.

Linc stared at the picture. She looked like she didn't have one care in the entire world. Her smile was breathtaking.

SHIT!

He pressed the call button.

Please answer.

"You've reached Alexis Hewson. I'm sorry I missed your call. Please leave a message, and I will call you back as soon as the game is over."

"It's me. I'm too drunk to drive back over to your place tonight but we need to talk. Call me back. Please."

She's not going to call you back tonight.

Another swig of Jack.

"Dude, nothing is getting fixed tonight. Let it go."

...

Breaking the surface of the water after a night with Jack was a rude awakening. The water allowed Linc to slide in, but the force around his body reminded him of its power. He glided to the surface for a breath of air and relaxed where things made the most sense. The world quickly slipped away as he effortlessly churned out warm-up laps.

Several laps into his swim, Linc felt a change in the water. Without looking, he knew other swimmers had entered the pool. Being early had afforded him the quiet he had gotten used to during spring break. Today, he welcomed the normalcy. Anything to keep his thoughts of Alexis at bay.

Linc paused at the side of the pool to watch the swimmer two lanes over from him. "Pierce, you're bringing your arm up too high again. Relax your wrists."

Swimming halfway down the pool and returning, Linc replicated Pierce's error. "I did your stroke on the way back. See the difference?"

"Yeah, man. Thanks. Will you watch me do a lap or two?" Pierce asked.

Linc had already planned on sticking around. "Sure."

"Awesome," he said, as he shot off the wall.

Drops of water raced down Linc's body as he climbed out of the pool to walk the lane and watch Pierce's laps. He glanced at the pace clock at mid-pool.

Hmmmmm. Wonder if Alexis is wake yet? Is she ever going to answer your calls?

Linc's eyes followed Pierce through the water, but found himself a million miles away. Or rather two miles, right back in Alexis' apartment. A fluffy white bed. A bare leg beneath a silky gown.

Shit!

He refocused on Pierce, but seconds later, he had floated back to Alexis. The pool had been his best attempt to escape the fact that he hadn't had any contact from her in two days, yet the minute his body was freed of the clutches of the rippled water, she filled his mind.

Pierce was looking at Linc at the edge of the pool, and from the lines in Pierce's forehead, he was waiting for feedback on his stroke. Linc wished he had feedback to give.

He cleared his throat and said to him, "Two more laps. Let's go."

Without question, Pierce pushed off the wall to complete the requested laps. Linc knelt down to concentrate on Pierce's form.

Close your fingers, hands downward, arm position, and keep your feet together. Always keep your feet together.

As Pierce turned at the far end of the pool and started back, Alexis swam into Linc's thought's like a mermaid seducing a sailor.

Watch where he's breathing.

Someone tapped Linc on the shoulder.

Izzie was staring down at him. "It's time we talked. Coach's office?"

Linc nodded. This was a conversation he'd been avoiding.

Excellent! You need this right now! Let's talk about your future while you don't have any of your shit together.

"Absolutely," he said.

"Linc! Did you see anything?" Pierce called out from his starting point.

"Think about your thumbs as they enter the water. Don't forget to really follow through on the push. And, you've gotta relax during recovery. Pierce, you know how to perform the stroke, now work out how to fly through the water."

Izzie laughed. "He can say that now after a thousand hours in the pool. Let's go."

Walking through the silent locker room, Linc grabbed a towel from the stack and dried off. He took a deep breath and pushed Alexis as far back in his mind as he could and headed to Coach's office.

The office was empty when he walked in. Izzie must have been stopped on the way. He had been in Coach's office countless times in the last four years, but for some reason the office suddenly felt smaller.

Linc had asked Coach once why he stored all the trophies, medals, and team pictures in a display case in the center of the IM building instead of in his office like most of the other Big Ten coaches.

"All that memorabilia is for the students to admire. To celebrate." He had tapped on the sliding wall of glass that opened up to a walkway above the pool and pointed." This is my trophy. My kids."

Back then, Linc didn't get it. The words had seemed bigger than him. But looking out from Coach's office now, he realized this was where the nuts and bolts of the team were put together.

Two weeks ago, Linc had started the mental countdown on how many days he had left to swim in these pools, be part of the team, and feel the sense of support of Izzie "The Enforcer" before finding his way as a teacher and coach. Then came the offer. Then he met Alexis.

Today, he contemplated stopping that countdown to be with a woman that hadn't returned his calls in two days.

Come on. Get your shit together for this meeting.

CHAPTER 32

Izzie walked into the office wearing a Michigan State tee shirt and shorts and sat down behind Coach's big metal desk. Linc rewrapped the towel covering his wet speedo. During his time on the team, a damp suit and towel had been standard attire for impromptu office meetings. This meeting felt different.

Well, that's why you got up here first.

"Have a seat," Izzie said, looking through a teetering stack of manila folders. "I know you're in here somewhere."

Linc slid into the same seat he had sat in during his first meeting with Coach. Butterfliers had been instructed to sit on the left and breast strokers on the right. No one knew why it mattered, but it was never questioned.

"Ha!" Izzie pulled a file out of the desk drawer. "Found it."

Linc moved the chair closer to the edge of the desk.

This is it. What are you going to do?

"Coach asked me to talk to you about the job. You've mentioned a couple of interviews with schools, but you haven't said much about our offer. Is State off the table for you at this point?"

Linc blinked at the question.

That was blunt.

An offer letter had been mailed to his house a few weeks ago, but he was certain he had until after graduation to give them an answer.

Dude, you talked to Grace about it.

"I thought I had until after graduation to decide."

Be real. You know you're not leaving Alexis.

Izzie flipped the file open and scanned to the second page. "Technically, you do. Linc, you know the swim program is not in the habit of making offers to swimmers within the program. Coach felt you were the right fit for this team and a great addition to the staff. But if your interests are in teaching, we'd like to get a jump on filling the position that's been reserved for you."

Linc stretched his right arm across the front of his body, and then used his left wrist to push his elbow in to extend the stretch. He repeated the same on the other side.

You need more time.

He wiped his sweaty hands on the stiff fibers of the towel. "If I was going to choose today, I'd stay here. That said, I still have some stuff to work out in my head."

Izzie smiled. "And, we don't want to rush the decision. I've noticed–

A freshman barged into the office carrying a piece of paper.

"Oh!" The swimmer stepped back surprised, and looked at his watch. "Coach said I'm supposed to watch tapes. I–"

"You're fine." Izzie popped up. "I've cued them up for you. Linc, meet me in the team room?"

Linc nodded and stood to leave.

"I'll be down in just a minute. I just want to make sure he's all set."

Linc thought about the first thing Izzie had ever said to him.

"No parents, or just general a lack of approval?"

He had responded the latter, and felt bad for saying so after.

After practice, he tried to go back to explain that his mother had loved him very much, but her hopes for him and his swimming career were set a bit higher than Michigan State.

Izzie had laughed and said, "Doesn't matter the reason, a lack of approval cuts deep. Let's get you in the pool and see if we can't make her eat her words."

Izzie was okay in Linc's book from then on. He had failed in the end. He knew it, and Izzie knew it. But she remained supportive of him from day one.

She walked into the team room through the women's locker room just as Linc had from the men's.

"Business concluded, agreed?" she asked.

"Agreed."

"So, Linc. What's the rule?"

"Come on. Are you serious?"

"Rule?"

"Every swimmer is entitled to a private life, until that life begins to drown the others in the pool. If at any point, a coach detects a problem and asks, the swimmer is obligated to discuss the issue with the coach or seek outside help if needed."

Izzie waited.

"But it's not like that," Linc stated reassuringly.

"Oh, this should be good. How is it, Linc?"

"I'm struggling with where and what to do next?"

She looked at him as if he had insulted her in the worst way possible. "Spill."

"It's the job decisions."

"Do not insult me, Linc."

He faced the seriousness of her eyes with his own.

Dude, she's got you. You are so screwed.

Linc sighed. "Fine. It's a girl."

Izzie laughed. "Isn't it always? And here I thought it was the weight of the offer."

"Not really fair here."

Throwing her hands in the air, Izzie surrendered. "True. I meant figuratively. Enlighten me."

"Her name is Alexis."

"Interesting. You stepped out of the pool for this one. What sport?"

Linc smiled sheepishly. "She's sort of the opposite of an athlete."

"So, what's the problem, Linc? She didn't fall under your spell, and it's throwing you off?"

What the hell?

Izzie laughed again. "Give me some credit. This isn't the first 'it's a girl' conversation I've had with one of you."

"No. She didn't fall for my charming personality, nor did I captivate her with my spell. In fact, I messed up, and she isn't speaking to me."

Linc walked around the pool table. "And, this room is so shitty."

"Yep, but you could've been on the scuba team. They don't even have a team room."

"You always say that."

"Well, Linc, one of you swimmers is always bitching about the conditions of this room," Izzie declared, sitting on one of the old sofas. "Funny, it's usually on the cusp of a serious conversation."

Whatever.

"You messed everything up..." she prompted.

Linc gathered the balls from the pockets of a hand-me-down pool table and racked them to delay the inevitable conversation. Selecting a stick off the wall, he walked to the end of the table and lined up the break.

"I like her a lot," Linc stated, as he hit the cue ball as hard as he could.

Balls splintered and rolled to all four corners of the table. A few found their way into the pockets, and Linc began making shot after shot without distinction between stripes or solids. Neither Izzie nor Linc said anything for several minutes.

"Linc."

He walked around the table searching for the next shot and struggling with what else to say. "She isn't like normal girls."

Izzie laughed.

Linc took aim again. "She's not talking to me because I wouldn't sleep with her."

Two balls crashed with violence, and then one dropped into a pocket with a dull thud.

"Are you sure that's why she isn't speaking with you?"

"Yeah. I'm sure."

"Why?"

Linc looked at Izzie. "Why what?"

"Why wouldn't you sleep with her?" Izzie grabbed a pool stick and took her time locating her first shot. "You said you liked her."

Dude, you didn't want to mess it up.

"For that reason, she's special."

"There are lots of reasons for waiting to have sex. Although, if my memory serves me correctly, you and the volleyball player got hot and heavy quick enough." She hit the cue ball squarely into the solid orange, and it sunk into the corner pocket. "I guess I'm missing something. I still don't understand why she's not talking to you."

"I was at her apartment two days ago, she wanted to have sex, and I said 'no.' She kicked me out, and I haven't heard from her since."

"Oh? And does Alexis know it's different?"

The solid purple found the left center pocket.

Linc shook his head. "I tried to tell her as she was kicking me out."

"Huh. Let me see if I got this straight. You like this girl..." Izzie raised her eyes to meet Linc's with a questioning stare.

"Alexis. Yes."

"You were at her apartment, and she came on to you, basically wanting to be intimate with you, and you turned her down..."

"Yes, but–"

She held up her hand. "You chose that moment to explain to her how you don't want to be with her, and that she's special."

"Shit, I should've talked to her before this."

I've totally messed this up.

"Kind of, yeah. That was your mistake if you like her as much as it sounds like you do." Izzie walked around the table and paused for Linc to move so she could go after the last ball in play. "This wasn't your brightest moment."

Linc picked up the rack from the side of the table.

As the eight ball fell, Izzie asked, "What are you going to do to fix it?"

"I'm not. I'm done. I haven't heard from her in two days."

You're not done. You're so not walking away.

Izzie laughed. "You're so not walking away. Rack'em."

Linc collected the balls, rolled them into shape and slipped the triangle over the group, and then dropped the loose ones into the rack with light thuds. Even as he worked each one into place, he pondered what he could do to fix the situation with Alexis.

As Izzie drew her stick back to shoot from the other end of the table, she asked, "What makes her different from the other girls you've dated?"

The cue rammed the waiting balls.

"Alexis doesn't care that I'm a swimmer. Or that I have money. She's incredibly driven and focused on her own goals. She cuts through the bullshit. She's real."

Izzie followed the balls as they scattered. "I guess I don't understand the problem."

"I don't want to hit it and quit it. I really like her."

"What do the guys think?"

Linc never saw the question coming.

He placed his pool stick back in the wall rack and took a seat on one of the sofas.

"That's an interesting question," he started. "Harrison calls her a charity case. Mikey's a bit more supportive, but..."

"A charity case?"

"Alexis isn't athletic. She doesn't fit the mold for the kind of girls Harrison thinks we should date."

"Plus-sized?"

"She's just Alexis to me. She's bigger than the other girls I've dated, but she's perfect the way she is."

"Is that why you turned her down?"

Hell NO!

"No."

"Are. You. Sure?" His coach was serious.

"Very."

Izzie softened. "Did you explain to her that you had feelings for her prior to the other night and how you want this to proceed?"

"Really, do we need to have this discussion?"

Izzie smiled. "Nope, you can continue to be a rock in the pool and get in the way of everyone out there."

"Harsh."

"Accurate."

"Fine. No, I never broke it down. We never actually had a conversation about a relationship."

"Advice time." Izzie took a shot and pocketed a couple of balls. "Go find her. Talk to her and explain how you feel. Do it now."

"That's it? This is the wisdom you're bestowing on me?"

She attacked the next shot from the other side of the table, and another ball landed softly into a pocket.

"Seems better than walking through the day hoping she calls. How's that worked for you?" Izzie examined the table as she continued. "Tell her you fucked up royally and ask for forgiveness. We love that."

Dude, you are totally going to ask for forgiveness.

"Linc, before you go find her and grovel, be certain you didn't reject her for more than you're saying. If you aren't one hundred percent sure about how you feel about Alexis, walk away. She'll have a difficult enough time in life without an asshole like you stringing her along."

WOW.

"You're on my side, right?" Linc wondered aloud, as he watched Izzie sink two more balls.

She looked up and smiled.

"It's hard to tell."

CHAPTER 33

The streets felt empty as Linc made his way to the coffee shop. Crazy that he went there, but he needed to feel close to her even if she wasn't at their table.

"Hey, Linc. How are you?" JoAnne asked, in a sympathetic tone.

"Same. Haven't heard from her. Has she been in yet today?"

JoAnne slowly shook her head. "Can I get you something?"

"Yeah. Anything but a vanilla latte." He forced a smile. "Something strong."

"Coming right up."

Even the four fives on a five dollar bill didn't shake his mood. Linc held it out toward JoAnne, but she waved him off.

"My treat today."

"You sure?"

"Yep."

Linc walked over and sat at the table that he and Alexis had sat at so many times since getting to know each other.

You were so suspicious in the beginning. What were you so afraid of? Getting hurt? No one's immune.

JoAnne placed a drink on the table.

As the door swung open, Linc heard his friends' voices and cringed. JoAnne walked away.

"Linc. Shit, man, you living here now?" Harrison asked. "Where's Charity?"

"Fuck off!"

"What's going on? You look like someone ran over your cat." Mikey sat down in Alexis' seat.

"I still haven't heard from Alexis." Linc slowly turned the coffee cup. "Not one returned message."

"Linc, don't be a pussy," Harrison said. "There's fat chicks everywhere."

Linc's fist knocked Harrison out of his chair and sent coffee flying everywhere.

"Her name is Alexis! One more fucking word about her, and I will finish this."

"Okay, Linc. He's sorry and a fucking idiot. Aren't you, Harrison?" Mikey picked up the chair and the coffee cup.

"Sorry, Linc. Jeez," Harrison mumbled, as he wiped blood from his nose. "I'm out."

JoAnne wiped the spilled coffee off the table.

"Sorry, JoAnne," Linc said quietly.

"Linc, well worth the cleanup. He's a dick."

"He can be," Mikey responded, laughing. "I guess I better go make sure you didn't break his nose."

Linc nodded. JoAnne sat down across from him.

"Okay, I wasn't supposed to tell you this today, but..." She glanced at the big wall clock.

"Not supposed to tell me what?"

"Alexis is leaving." JoAnne held her hands up. "Chill, I'm going to tell you. The internship she interviewed for in Chicago called, and they wanted her to start sooner rather than later."

"Wait...What? That's not possible. She never told me."

"Yeah, I know. She wasn't going to take it. She fell for you pretty hard. Then, all of a sudden, she said it would be a mistake not to take this opportunity. She never told me what happened between you. She just said she made a mistake to think it was real."

"It's real."

JoAnne touched Linc's arm. "I believe you, Linc."

"I can't believe she'd leave without saying anything. We never talked after..."

He knew JoAnne was waiting for him to finish his sentence, but he wasn't going to.

"Her train doesn't leave until 11:35." JoAnne said slowly, with another quick glance at the clock. "You've got time."

Linc kissed JoAnne on top of the head and ran out of the coffee shop.

...

As Linc slid the car into park, he scanned the empty cup

holders and remembered the last time he had parked in this parking lot. Two vanilla lattes...one extra hot with a double cup. So many things had changed in the weeks since he'd picked Alexis up from the train station.

He opened the door and, climbing out, his eyes glided over the area seeking the woman who had been the focus of his life for the last few weeks. The woman who had helped him find direction. The woman who had helped him change.

Alexis!

Linc paused to study the woman who had captured his thoughts from the first moment he had heard her laugh. There was the woman who had given so much. The woman would give up so much to be with him.

"I want to see the world. I want to be that person that has so many stamps that I have to have additional passports. I want to conquer the world. Asia Minor is my future destination."

Her dreams. Her goals. Her need to explore the world. Never any mention of exploring love. A soon-to-be high school swim coach was not in her carefully constructed plans.

Linc got back into the car and leaned his head against the seat.

A train whistle rang out. Moments later, the train pulled to a stop before the people who waiting to board. Alexis quickly moved to board. As her foot touched the first step, she paused and looked in his direction.

Linc gripped the car handle.

You're already gone, Pretty.

Alexis climbed the steps out of sight.

Linc waited for the train to pull off. He wasn't exactly sure why. Maybe he was waiting to see if Alexis would get off the train and come to him. Maybe he needed to watch her disappear to realize she was truly gone. Maybe he needed time to pull his shit together before returning to life without her in it.

A text alert sounded, and Linc's heart stopped. He reached into his pocket for his phone. His lungs had seized too hard to breathe.

Grace: Word of the day...fanfaronade.

Linc threw the phone across the car.

As the train left the station, so did he.

Acknowledgements

Thank you … Coach Matt Gianiodis, Coach Kathleen Milloy, Coach Eric Best, and the entire Michigan State swim team for allowing me to crash your practice and ask tons of questions. #Congratsonthenewpool #FreshmengirlsthanksforUberingwithme

Thank you … Kellen Beckwith for laying the foundation of my swimming knowledge and explaining 'gently' that Denison is better than MSU. I hope I got the swim stuff right.

Thank you … Parents for the unwavering love and support you've provided me. Mom, I promise to write a story with a loving 'mother – daughter' relationship soon. Dad, I look forward to you pointing out the inaccuracies in this book. Most of all, I appreciate your understanding when I disappear to focus on my writing.

Thank you … brother for working so hard to change the world and answering my calls almost all the time.

Thank you … brother for making me think outside the box and making me laugh like no one else on earth.

Thank you … Noble for welcoming me into your life.

Thank you … sisters and niece for balancing the sexes in the family. #GIRLPOWER

Thank you … grandparents, aunts, uncles, and cousins for helping to shape me into the person I've become.

Thank you … Erika and Troy for taking care of my monsters and me so I could focus all my attention on writing.

Thank you … Richelle for being Richelle. You've been involved with every step of this book. Everyone needs that person that will say 'That sucks' – she's mine. #everythingcantbebestever

Thank you … Angie, Eden, Sadie, Al, Louise, Amber, Freya,

Angel, Petra and Roy, Alice, RB, Dawn, Noelle, Christina, Abby, Tracy, Ellie, Isabelle, Connie, Kyleigh, Rod and Sharon, Cat, J.Witt, Meredith, Julie, Jessica, Hannah, Kara, Lisa, Sarah, Allison, Audrey, Jenna, Emily, Courtney, Krista, Lindsey, Rachel, Gina, and Katrina.

Thank you … Brittany Gibbons and CGG for giving me a magical place. It's not a location; it's a state of mind.

Thank you … betas for your insight and honesty. Your dedication to providing thoughtful feedback while worrying about the author's feelings shows the love you have for this community. Never change.

Thank you … bloggers for tirelessly spreading the word about *Before Him Comes Me* and, now, *In the Pursuit of Charity*. From small blogs with fifty followers to super blogs with 100,000+, you are responsible for connecting new authors with new readers and you work tirelessly to accomplish that goal.

Thank you … readers for not coming to my house and choking me at the conclusion of this story. When my mom finished the book, she immediately said, 'NO! I demand a happy ending.' The next morning, she called again. 'I need a happy ending. What about the dog, Gage?' My point is, you're not the only one who wanted to choke me.

Good news, this is a prequel.

Seriously, thank you very much for putting up with my long delay between books and for giving this read a chance. Keep going, there's more …

About the Author

Alexandria Sure is from Michigan and adores her supportive family, her two rescue pups, and her mighty Spartans. Her coffee obsession leads her to writing in local coffee shops where characters come alive between salted caramel lattes and large cups of "cold brew extra cream two Splenda," which are usually on the counter when she walks in because the baristas know her car. (Thanks, Biggby!)

When she is not writing, she spends a great deal of her time perfecting her craft. She is an active member of Capital City Writers Association and attends several writing conferences each year.

Sure's first novel, *Before Him Comes Me*, is an unconventional romance of self-discovery, described by readers as "the first BDSM book with no sex."

Excerpt from

Complex Deflection

Vivian clutched a key she had pulled from the glovebox of her car until the key's teeth bit into her fingers. The vision of her family home blurred as tears collected in the corners of her eyes. She went anyway. The weight of entering this house again rooted the wooden door to the ground as Vivian forced it open. The smell of woodsy pine met her like someone waiting for her inevitable return.

"Get over yourself." Vivian's words traveled around the entryway and back again. A deafening silence returned as her words evaporated. In the hallway, Vivian eased past a table that faced the wall of framed photographs. Without a glance, she hurried by the dated design of the formal living room, dining room, and kitchen in order to find refuge in her sanctuary. At the bottom of the stairs, Vivian paused to let the lightness of the space fill her.

Tears she had been holding in for the last hour threatened to escape. Shaking her head in disgust, a flash of brown caught her eye. Vivian creeped into the living area and stared out the glass door.

A man stood in the backyard. Vivian moved to the window and saw it again...a flash of brown. It was a big, brown dog and it stopped at the stranger's feet. The guy threw a yellow ball and the dog was off again. Vivian watched the man toss the ball once more before she remembered she was not the one trespassing.

"Super. What is that like three football fields away?" she said sarcastically, as she opened the sliding door and made her way toward the stranger. She hadn't stepped on the grass since her eighth birthday party. "Kind of thought this was all for looks."

She was halfway to the stranger when the dog suddenly bolted at her.

"Henry! Stop!" the man ordered.

The dog stopped. Vivian stopped as well. Her hair stuck to the back of her neck, and a rogue droplet of sweat inched its way down her scalp as she stood waiting for the next instruction.

"Henry! Sit!"

While the man approached, the dog, his tail wagging wildly, had trouble staying seated. The man extended a hand to Vivian, but she was still fixated on the dog.

"Henry. Come."

The dog raced to the feet of the man and sat down, his eyes on his owner.

"Can I–" Vivian finally looked up at the man who was trespassing on her property, and then was momentarily lost by the way his eyes danced in the light. To say he was attractive would be like saying a fish can swim. There was something more about him. He was beautiful. And, Vivian had never considered a man to be beautiful.

The dog nudged the man's hand.

"This is Henry. Actually, King Henry." He said as he pet the dog's head.

"Can I pet him?" Vivian asked, trying to not stare though she was already half lost in the deep green of the man's eyes.

"He'd love it." He kneeled down to pet Henry. "Are you here to look at the property?"

Vivian tilted her head a bit to see if his words made more sense that way. They didn't. But then, as if a switch had been turned on, Vivian responded, "I live here. This is my house."

"Really." He stood and looked back at the house. "We thought it was empty."

"I've been away."

"Awkward," Vivian heard him say under his breath, then louder, he said, "Great yard."

Vivian waited.

The man looked embarrassed at the situation. She didn't respond. He bent down to pick up the two balls on the ground. Henry was up with his eyes locked on the hand with the balls. "Henry loves ..."

Vivian turned to see what had snatched Henry's attention away from the lure of the balls to stand at attention facing her house.

A taller, male version of her was walking briskly from the sliding glass door with a concerned look on his face.

"Viv, are you alright?" he asked.

"Yeah, I'm fine." Vivian crossed her arms. As the man reached them, she continued, "This is–I'm sorry. I don't know your name."

"Gus."

"Gus?" Viviana eyed him dubiously. He didn't look like a Gus. Like a plumber?

Gus nodded. "Yep, Gus."

"Gus, this is Branden, my brother."

"Nice to meet you." Gus said, with a nod.

"He was playing with his dog when I–"

Branden dismissed him without another glance. "We need to talk."